The Gaia Project

The Gaia Collection Book 2

Claire Buss

To, Agnieszka
Thank-you so much
for your support and
encouragement x.

Claire Buss

Published by CB Visions in 2019

Second Edition

www.cbvisions.weebly.com

Cover artwork by Ian Bristow

In a board room, behind closed doors...

'What's the status of City 42?'

'The revolt is over and Anti-Corp have been destroyed yet...'

'Yet what?'

'The city is not in our hands. An independent governance has been set up, headed by Martha Hamble.'

'Hamble? Hamble? I know that name. Isn't she already a director on our Board?'

'That's the father, Ma'am. But he was a victim of the Anti-Corp riots. Martha's his daughter.'

'Well, that's alright then, isn't it? She's one of us, isn't she?'

'Apparently not, Ma'am.'

'Why do I know her name then?'

'She was one of those affected by the anomalous medical condition.'

'Successfully?'

'No, Ma'am. She carried the child to term and completed a natural pregnancy.'

'Ah. What about the others afflicted?'

'Dina Grey successful miscarried while Ruth Maddocks went to term and completed pregnancy.'

'Wasn't there a fourth?'

'Yes, Ma'am. Ingrid Jenkins. She died in the Anti-Corp terrorist attack on Corp Tech. Medical claimed termination.'

'And there haven't been anymore?'

'Not according to our sources, Ma'am.'

'Well that's something, I suppose. What about the baby labs?'

'Permanently closed. The new governor discovered the production and sale and decided to shut down the supply chain. So far, efforts to re-establish the product line have been unsuccessful.'

'But we have someone on the inside?'

'Yes, Ma'am.'

'Is there anything else I need to know?'

'A small cult has formed, Ma'am. Worshipping Gaia, the Spirit of the Earth. There's been some effigy, but I don't think we have anything to worry about.'

'Ah yes, the blue lady phenomenon. When we take back control order repainting where necessary.'

'What about medical and food supplies? Should we reconnect the city?'

'No, not yet. We cannot allow the success of any leadership outside of Corporation. Which reminds me, have the plans for City 15 been carried out?'

'Everything is in hand, Ma'am.'

'Excellent. Keep me informed.'

Chapter 1

'I'm worried about Jed,' Kira said as she faced the vid-screen in front of her. It was meant to be synth-caf with the girls but lately it was physically difficult for them to all be in the same place at once. As it was, only Dina had linked into the comm. They were still waiting for Ruth and Martha to appear.

'Why? What's happened? Has he been getting into more fights at work?' Dina sounded sincere but she was fiddling with something off camera, her attention not fully on Kira or the conversation.

'Oh no, nothing like that, he's just not himself. And he has a meeting with his boss today. He thinks they're going to force him to get a new partner, but he says he can't think about it, not since...' Kira trailed off.

'Not since losing his sister and Pete.' Dina had stopped whatever she was doing and was looking straight at Kira. 'You've done everything you can for him you know. Grief is a difficult thing for people to process.'

'But it's been months. So much else has happened.' Kira looked at Dina with pleading eyes. 'I need him. I need you, all of you. I feel like I'm always all on my own.'

'I know, I'm sorry. There's so much to do here, I never seem to have a spare five minutes.' Dina looked away from the screen, her attention momentarily elsewhere. 'Huh. Thought I saw a bee.' She turned back to Kira. 'We've got bees here; did I tell you?'

'Yeah. I've been thinking I should come out to Camp Eden. Bring Grace with me. It would be good to see Max again, have a look at what you guys are getting up to out there. Visit the bees and everything.' Kira tried not to sound too desperate, but she wanted a change of scenery. Besides if there were bees at Camp Eden, maybe Kira would see Gaia as well.

'Yes! You should totally come. It would be great to see you.' Dina was grinning widely at the camera. There was a shout behind her, and she whipped her head round, half rising from the chair. 'Oh wow - sorry Kira, I've got to go. They've spotted something in the trees, some kind of cat. It's so exciting. Catch up with you soon.' The connection went dead.

Kira sighed at the blank screen in front of her. So much for synth-caf with the girls. She was about to turn her comm link off when Martha's face blinked into view.

'Sorry I'm late. I can only stay for five minutes but I wanted to drop in and say hi to you all.' She looked puzzled. 'Where is everyone?'

'Hi, Ma. Dina had to go, they found a cat or something. And Ruth, well, Ruth hasn't turned up yet,' Kira replied, glad to see her friend but annoyed that she was already talking about going.

'That's odd. Ruth didn't tell me she had other plans. At least, I don't think she did.' Martha frowned. 'Kira, I am so tired. I don't know whether I'm coming or going half the time. I've got another meeting in a few minutes, more problems with supplies and I have no idea how we're going to sort this one out.'

Kira took pity on her friend. 'You'll figure it out, Ma, you always do.'

'Thanks, Kira. Look I've got to go but let's try and have dinner soon. We should get all the kids together as well. Ruth said Lucas was trying to crawl yesterday. I can't believe how much time has flown by.' Martha gave a little wave and disconnected her feed before Kira even had chance to agree to the dinner plans. It didn't matter anyway; they were always saying they would make plans but somehow never found the time to actually put them in the diary.

Kira realised that Martha had an important job. She was governor of City 42 and since the Anti-Corp rebellion had removed much of the previous administration, Martha had faced a huge job putting in new procedures and finding staff capable of carrying out

5

her orders. They'd managed to fix the water problem with the nearby river supply and the combined effort of the city's inhabitants had repaired the old sewage works so that clean water came in and dirty water was recycled. Thank goodness Archive had all the records on how the system worked. Without the board members of Corporation to provide the passcodes so many of the city's systems were locked out. The food hydrators still worked but processed sachets were running low, as were medical supplies. No-one seemed to know where or how to get more.

Kira waited a few more minutes in front of the blank screen but there was no sign of Ruth. She pinged her comm, no answer. Since having her baby, Ruth had shrunk into herself. She'd stopped teaching full time in order to look after Sarah, and take care of Lucas for Martha, but she was still liaison for Academy which meant attending various government meetings as well. When Kira did occasionally see her, Ruth was quieter, made less of an effort with her appearance and frequently missed catch ups like these. Turning off the screen, Kira decided to go and see Ruth at the apartment she shared with Martha. Make sure she was alright. She needed to talk to someone about Gaia. She hadn't seen any signs of the goddess for months. There was no talk of a blue lady on the sweeps and Kira wanted to know if any of her friends had seen something, anything. It felt strange that their lives had been so influenced by the spirit of the Earth yet now when they needed guidance more than ever before, she was nowhere to be found.

How did you even go about trying to find a spirit or god or whatever she was? The only thing Kira knew for sure was that too many people had seen Gaia for her to only be a figment of imagination. She went to get Grace ready to go out, determined to speak to at least one of her friends, in person.

DING: Latest species discovered in Camp Eden - Felis silvestris - a beautiful cat. Check out the images at CE's holopage.

It was lunchtime by the time Kira arrived at Ruth's door. Grace had decided she was hungry, then produced an explosive nappy which had required Kira to change the baby's outfit. She had then rushed to get Grace into her travel cube before she fell asleep. Kira felt harassed as she flashed her ident in order to gain access to Martha and Ruth's apartment block. Since Martha became governor and Dina had moved out to Camp Eden there had been lots of changes in their living arrangements. Kira often felt sad that her friends weren't the other side of the door, like it had been back when they had all shared a flat but, she knew it made sense for Martha to be seen as a person of importance and to live in a secure, elite, apartment block. At least she wasn't alone, she had Ruth with her.

There was no answer when Kira knocked on the door, so she let herself in. Martha had keyed entry to Kira and Dina in case of emergencies.

'Ruth? Ruth - are you here? It's Kira.' There was no answer, but the cry of a baby echoed down the hallway quickly followed by another.

'Oh, for frag sake! You've woken them up!' Ruth yelled then appeared in a doorway holding her baby girl, Sarah and Martha's baby boy, Lucas. They were both screaming.

'I'm sorry. I was worried about you...' But Kira couldn't hear herself think over the screams of the babies, so she hurried to take Lucas and was surprised when Ruth handed her both children. Kira glanced over at Grace to make sure she was still alright, glad she'd remembered to put the soundproofing on the travel cube. She was fast asleep. The babies stopped crying immediately, both children liked Kira and she held them close to her body, rocking herself and shushing to them.

'That never works for me,' Ruth said bitterly, glaring at Kira.

Kira looked at her friend. Ruth's hair looked unbrushed and matted in places. She had dark shadows under her eyes, her skin was pale, and her shoulders slumped in defeat. 'Why didn't you vid me?' Kira asked softly. 'I could've come over, helped out.'

'Unless you can take over completely what's the point? It's the same mind-numbing grind, day in - day out. Half an hour here or there does nothing. I'm supposed to be at this meeting later and...' Ruth stopped talking as sobs started to escape.

Kira looked around for somewhere to put the children and saw a play cube in the living area. She gently placed both babies inside then set up a sensory loop to keep them entertained. Gentle music began to play accompanied by soft lights and shapes that moved across the cube walls. Kira went into the kitchen and made some synth-caf. She put all the dirty crockery into the steam washer and checked the fridge for baby milk. There was nothing prepared so she started a new batch. 'When did you last eat?' she asked Ruth.

Ruth shrugged her shoulders. Kira wondered if her friend even knew what day of the week it was. She looked in the cupboards. There wasn't much in there, but she found a couple of sachets of nutrient rich meals and activated them in the food hydrator. Then she steered her friend towards a chair and put a hot meal and drink in front of her.

'Eat,' Kira said and gestured at the untouched food. Ruth looked at it and shook her head.

'I don't have much of an appetite these days.' But she did as Kira asked, picking up a fork and toying with the food.

'Ruth, I do appreciate how hard it is having a baby, you know. Let me help you, please.'

Ruth stayed quiet.

Kira tried again. 'Look, I know I didn't go through labour like you did but I have had Grace since her birth. I know how tiring the constant crying can be, what sleepless nights feel like, the non-stop merry-go-round of bottle feeding, washing clothes, making more bottles and changing nappies. I do know how you feel.'

Ruth stared at Kira but still didn't speak.

'It feels like it'll never end but it does get easier, I promise.' Kira gave a small laugh. 'Either that or you finally get the hang of it. I know it's hard, believe me I do, but you have to start taking better care of yourself as well.'

Ruth snorted. 'How am I supposed to find the time to do that? Looking after Sarah and Lucas is a lot harder than looking after one, Kira. You have no idea how tired I am. And Martha is at work all the time, I get no help. I'm trying so hard to not rely on technology but it's ridiculous, I get no time for myself at all. Surely it shouldn't be this hard?' She shoved a spoonful of food into her mouth and avoided Kira's gaze.

Kira stayed quiet. She knew it was hard raising a child. Late night feeds and early morning wake up calls took it out of you. But she also knew that Martha had tried to hire night nannies and Ruth had point blank

9

refused to accept what she termed *outside help*. The two friends sat in silence, one screaming silently for help but not knowing how to ask for it, the other wishing she knew what to do to make things better.

'What time is your meeting?' asked Kira once Ruth had finished eating.

'I'm not sure, I was going to feed the children and then take them to the office crèche. I think I've got all the reports I'm supposed to have.'

'Why don't I feed Lucas, you can do Sarah, and I'll walk with you over to Hamble HQ,' offered Kira.

Ruth smiled in thanks and went to get the children.

MSCHILD: *Protest tomorrow in the Main Square. Bring back lab babies. Natural doesn't work!*

ANON17: *Never mind babies. Bring back Corp! Bring back Corp! Bring back Corp!*

ENCRYPTED MESSAGE FROM NEW CORP TO 7421
>>STATUS REPORT DUE - UPDATE ON THE FOLLOWING:
1. FORCE
2. RESUPPLY
3. BABY LABS
4. PROPAGANDA<<

ENCRYPTED MESSAGE FROM 7421 TO NEW CORP
>>*1. The new Security Guard measures have been accepted and implemented. The power shift within Force has begun but Minkov has forced a loophole. He's made Jed Jenkins Captain of the City Guard - we will have no jurisdiction over him.*
2. Resupply is still blocked. No-one has managed to figure out the required codes. Supplies are low and will soon become critical.
3. Governor Hamble refuses to reinstate the baby labs. They remain inactive.
4. The use of anonymous sweeps is working well, support is wavering.
Additional question - what about City 15?<<

ENCRYPTED MESSAGE FROM NEW CORP TO 7421
>>REPORT RECEIVED.
UNFORTUNATE DEVELOPMENTS AT FORCE BUT THEY WILL BE DEALT WITH. QUESTION NOTED. STAND BY FOR FURTHER INSTRUCTION<<

Chapter 2

C42N: Do we need Security Guards and Force? Crime is down. Do you feel safe? Join the virtual conversation in social hub beta.

SMAC: New Security Guards are local representatives from your community working together with Force. They're here to keep you safe.

ANON17: What about old Force? Who's watching them?

Jed watched the latest squad of security guards walk down the corridor. It was a new initiative from the governor's office. A mixture of security guards and Force operatives would work together to keep the peace, the idea being that the security guards were representatives from the community and therefore more in touch with daily citizen life. At least that's what Sean MacIntyre, aide to the governor, had told everyone on the daily sweeps. It seemed to Jed that the governor's office was trying to complicate a justice system that worked perfectly fine, but he could see how involving citizens was a good idea.

'You wanted to see me, Boss?' Jed asked as he poked his head around the office door of Tony Minkov, Chief of Force. Since losing Pete, Jed had no patience for the other detectives on Force and had come to blows several times. This had earnt him three official warnings and the threat of unpaid leave in order to attend anger management sessions. But Jed didn't think he'd upset anyone recently, so he had no idea why he was being called in.

'Yes, come in, Jenkins. Sit, sit.' The chief fiddled with his handheld and scratched his head before clearing his throat loudly. 'Things are changing here in City 42. It's happening slowly but it won't be long before old timers like me are pushed out the door and Force changes into something else.' He glanced up and saw the incredulous look on Jed's face. 'No, hear me out, Jenkins. I don't like it. My gut is telling me we need to watch our backs. I need someone I can trust and rely on to look after our city as we see these changes through. Someone who takes their civic duty seriously.' Minkov looked Jed directly in eye. 'The thing is, Jenkins, you're no good to me as a Detective.'

'But, Sir!' Jed protested. 'If this is about me not finding a new partner, I will, I promise. I just haven't found anyone yet. It's been... difficult.'

'It's been difficult for all of us, Jenkins,' Minkov spoke gruffly. In their own way, both men still mourned the loss of Detective Pete Barnes. 'But it doesn't change what needs to be done. I have detectives I can use on local crime. You I need on the other side. You are being promoted to Captain of the City Guard and will be in charge of a team of specialist operatives who will look to the safety of our citizens, our city and be responsible for any future exploration.'

'Future exploration? Isn't that Agent Devereaux's department?' asked Jed.

'Devereaux is on assignment in City 15 but his department has been downsized. Part of these new changes. All the agents have been reassigned elsewhere - another reason why I want you to head up this new division. I need someone with a level head, someone who knows the law, who cares about the city. We can't have a hothead in charge.'

'Do we need a city militia, Sir?' Jed was surprised at such an aggressive move; it wasn't the sort of thing he'd come to expect from Martha's governorship.

'It may seem extreme now, Jenkins, but I remember the City 15 riots and the violent backlash from Corporation. If we want to protect our independence, then we need the appropriate defenders and having you in charge puts my mind at ease.'

'You don't think Corporation still have a standing military, do you?' Jed had never considered the possibility before.

'I wouldn't put anything past them. The fact that we haven't heard anything from Corporation makes me nervous.' Chief Minkov tapped his badge. 'Force has always been a separate entity, we've always stood for truth and justice, working with whatever government has been in place yet our hands were tied without us even knowing thanks to Corporation lies. It's our job to protect City 42's freedom, Jenkins.'

'Yes, Sir. Of course, but, but... I'm still Force, aren't I?'

'Yes, but you report directly to Governor Hamble. Think of me as your counterpart on civilian matters.' Minkov watched closely to see how Jed would react. He thought it was a good idea to split Force, while he still had the power to implement change and could choose the right man for the job. Everything was in too much flux to continue with the old methodology. There had to be the capability for a greater show of force and indeed protection in case Corporation retaliated in some way. It was a distinct possibility that they would. The severe repercussions that happened in City 15 when they tried to shake off Corporation rule had been swift and brutal. It might seem quiet here in City 42 now, but it didn't mean things were going to stay that way.

Jed didn't need to think about it, he wanted a change. 'Thank you, Sir. I accept.'

Minkov held out his hand. 'Good man, you've made the right decision.' They shook. 'You need to report to Governor Hamble's office and get your briefing notes. That new fella, Sean Macinwotsit, should have all the details, but don't let him boss you around - you don't work for him and you certainly don't report to him. Did you get that background check in for him?'

Jed fished his handheld out of his pocket and tapped the screen a few times.

'Yes, Sir. Apparently, he spent some time studying in 15 before he and his parents moved here from City 9.' Jed had been surprised by that; he didn't think anyone had ever chosen to come to City 42 from City 9. He continued reading. 'Strong family ties with Corporation that go back several decades but since being here he hasn't shown any loyalty to Corp.' He looked up at the chief. 'Martha says he's fantastic at his job, she doesn't know what she'd do without him. He could be a runaway?'

'Hmm.' Minkov didn't look convinced. 'Keep an eye on him, Jenkins.'

'Yes, Sir. Will I still be based here, Sir? In my new

role?'

'Yes, for now. It makes sense to keep all the equipment and men together, but we can hash out the particulars later. I expect there will be some sort of official ceremony, after all this is a new role with more responsibility to take on.'

'Yes, Sir. I have a city meeting up at Hamble HQ now anyway so I can pick up the details while I'm there.'

The chief agreed and dismissed him.

Thinking to himself, Jed walked slowly out of the building. He felt strange, all his career he'd worked towards becoming a detective. Being partnered with Pete had felt like it was always meant to be. Since his friend had died, he had felt lost and adrift, unsure exactly of what his next move would be. He'd even considered leaving Force completely and retraining to do something else. Unusual but not unheard of. Now though, he felt like he had a purpose again. Being in charge of a city militia - it was different, but it felt like something he could get behind. Since cutting ties with Corporation, the city was alone and vulnerable. Jed needed to be in a position to help protect it and now he was. He strode off confidently to Hamble HQ, as the governor offices were affectionately known, to find out what his first assignment would be. He hoped there wouldn't be too much additional paperwork with this new role. That had always been something he had never been too keen on.

It was a short walk from Force to Hamble HQ. After the destruction of Corp Tech and the discontinuation of lab grown babies, Martha had decided to take over Collection Towers and base her government there. She had made sure that a representative from each area of the city had at least an office, if not an entire floor. Jed wove through the protesters who had started to gather in Main

Square. It was peaceful at the moment, but he made a mental note to ensure all operatives had their riot gear, just in case.

'ID.' One of the new security guards held out his hand for Jed's ident. It flashed green when scanned and the guard waved him through. Jed didn't recognise him, or the woman stationed further in the foyer. *They must both be new civilian recruits* he thought as he took the stairs up to Martha's offices. He was met by yet more security checks, this time he knew the staff and spent a few moments chatting with them. Everyone had lost someone in the terrorist attack on Corp Tech, so it had created a bond between those who'd worked the disaster site and those who'd come forward to work in the new government.

A quick look at Martha's office showed the door was firmly shut, keyed red for do not disturb so Jed tried his luck next door where Sean MacIntyre, Martha's aide, could usually be found. He was sitting at his desk frowning and looked up in alarm as Jed entered the room. His brow quickly cleared, and he swiped his screen blank.

'Everything alright?' asked Jed, nodding towards the desk.

'What? Oh that, yes, yes, nothing to worry about. What can I do for you, Detective? The city meeting isn't for another half an hour or so.'

'It's Captain now, Sean. I understand you have my briefing notes, for the City Guard?'

'Oh, oh right, I see. They made you, I mean you're the new... huh, I'd never have thought.' Sean scratched his head and then began opening drawers in his desk until he found the info jack he was looking for. 'Everything is on here,' he said passing the jack over.

'Congratulations, I guess. Hmm?'

'You seem surprised, Sean,' said Jed, bemused by the man's reaction.

'Yes! I mean, no. Of course not. It's just, you're a detective. Were a detective. And there were other candidates who were less... reactive. But you don't want to hear about that.' Sean pulled himself together and smiled at Jed. 'It will be great working with you, I'm sure.'

'U huh. What's my first assignment - do you know?'

'No. Well, maybe. I think it's straight in at the deep end to be honest. Governor Hamble will let you know soon, I'm sure. For now, get your team sorted out, be ready for anything, that sort of thing. You've got all the gear and everything. All the details about the City Guard's responsibilities are on that jack. If there's nothing else?' Sean had risen out of his seat and begun to usher Jed out of the office.

'I guess not. Thanks.' Jed looked at Martha's door again on his way past, but it was still closed. It would have been nice to get his new assignment from the governor directly, but he supposed she was busy getting ready for the city meeting. He'd go back to his old desk later and download the information he'd been given. He might even be able to wangle a new desk now. With half an hour to wait before the meeting was due to start, he got out his handheld to tell Kira the good news and noticed the sweeps had already got there. They never missed a trick.

ANON17: Who voted on city militia? I didn't!

FORCE: ***Official Announcement*** Detective Jed Jenkins has been promoted to Captain and will run the

18

new City Guard.

GOVHAM: *Congratulations to Captain Jenkins and the new City Guard. Together we're looking after City 42.*

ANON40: *Security Guards & Force City Guard. Overkill much?*

C42N: *Captain Jenkins is the new face of City 42's safety. Read more online!*

Chapter 3

C42N: Government meeting today. What should be the priority? Join the virtual conversation in social hub beta.

MSCHILD: How do we know they're not still selling babies behind our backs? Why won't they bring back Collection?

ANON17: More food! More food!

GOVHAM: We will release a city-wide update later today. Together we're looking after City 42.

ANON40: Bring back the force-field. Make us feel safe again.

CORPTECH2: Why is Corp Tech still closed? We need our jobs! We need our tech!

Martha's head hurt. The lack of sleep and the general weariness that came with being a new parent plus the brain numbing exhaustion of running City 42 was relentless. Trying to figure out the answers to problems she didn't even know existed until they were dumped on her desk. Like the first chilling discovery they had made after taking over from Corporation. The previous administration had been growing additional babies in the baby lab and selling them, elsewhere. With the collapse of the computer systems, Martha's team had yet to discover where and why the babies were being sold. It had shocked them all and of course the details had been leaked on the sweeps. There had been near riots but somehow Force had managed to contain the citizens anger, funnelling it towards clearing the debris from Corp Tech and establishing the new sewerage system. But finding out Corporation policies like that only added to her fears that she wasn't helping the people of her city enough, that she was letting them down when they needed her most.

It never stopped. Even when she did manage to get out of the office, her work followed her home, invading her attempts at privacy. Everyone knew where the new governor of City 42 lived. And no-one seemed to have any qualms about passing by to give their opinion on something, or complain about something or more often than not, have a gawp at Lucas, her natural baby.

Martha sifted through the urgent memos on her handheld. She was pleased to see Chief Minkov had made Jed's new role official. A memo reporting no new natural pregnancies caught her eye, despite the contaminated water supply having been replaced, the number of confirmed natural pregnancies had not exploded as expected. She moved that one to her recycle bin. In a way, no pregnancies were a good thing, considering the limitations of the city's food and medical resources. Martha cast an eye over the crop report from Camp Eden. They were growing food, but they couldn't supply the entire city overnight and anyway, she thought ruefully, many citizens distrusted the natural, organic food, preferring to use their food hydrators and dried sachets. Filing that report under Food she felt a twinge of panic, those packets wouldn't last forever, and supplies were running low. They needed to find a solution.

Rhythmic pounding joined the simmering ache in Martha's head. How could they have run so low? When Corporation had been in charge, the citizens of City 42 had never run out of vital medical supplies or food sachets. But there was no-one left to ask about supply and demand. The mob had lynched the Corporation board members six months ago and despite their best efforts to sift through the records left behind it wasn't clear exactly how re-supply occurred. When the board members had attempted to leave the city, they'd set their computer files to self-destruct and because the whole Corporation system was linked it had wiped out Martha's father's files as well. It was a disaster.

Martha's calendar pinged. At least the power was still running strong - everything was solar powered so they shouldn't have any issues with that. It wasn't like the sun was about to fall out of the sky. Martha sighed. She had a meeting with her advisors in five minutes. Among other things, Martha had requested a complete report on medical supplies and any potential issues, as well as ideas on how to solve those problems. After all the facts and the problems were coming from the people working in the medical centres, they should know what they needed as a priority and surely someone would come forward with information on how it was done in the past.

Medicine didn't magically appear, it had to have

been delivered one way or another. Martha rubbed her little blue Gaia statue for luck before heading out of the relative safety of her office and into the jaws of yet another meeting. They would get to the bottom of the supply issue, one way or another.

Entering the room Martha was pleased to see everyone was already there - Jed in his new role as Captain of the City Guard and as a representative from Force, Ruth as representative for Academy and supplying notes from Archive, and the Surgeon General of Med Centre, Dr William Lee. The Force chief didn't attend unless there was a vote and Ben Jenkins, the ex-Anti-Corp representative, had been side-lined to work as Martha's unofficial eyes and ears. He was happier reporting to her without an audience. Which meant the only absence was Agent Devereaux who was meant to be on assignment in City 15. Martha took her chair and smiled at Sean, as he handed her a cup of synth-caf. Martha tapped her handheld, ready to start the session but before she could speak the Surgeon General opened the meeting without any preamble.

'We've figured out why we aren't getting resupplied.'

Martha liked him immensely, no nonsense, straight to the point. She gestured for him to continue.

'There's a transporter pod in the basement, bloody alarm has been going off for weeks, but no-one knew what it was for.' He glanced around the table apologetically. 'Turns out this pod is used to move supplies between Corporation cities. All we need to do is enter the authorisation code and input our request.'

'Fantastic,' said Martha, feeling like things were finally going their way.

'Yes, well, it would be - if we knew what the authorisation code is.'

'What do you mean, you don't know? Someone must know it?' Ruth looked as knackered as Martha felt and had apparently forgotten to brush her hair that morning, luckily her unruly curls hid most of the damage.

'Turns out the code changed regularly and was given to the Med-Techs via Dr Basjere's office over in Science Division. We can't ask him because, well, because he's dead. None of the Med-Techs know where the code originated from. We've checked the computers but with no access passes we're completely locked out.'

'How bad are supplies getting?' Martha wasn't sure she wanted to know.

'We've got about another week, for patching up minor injuries. Thankfully no-one requires any kind of surgery at the moment because we are running low on things like plasma.' The Surgeon General looked down at the handheld in front of him to steady his nerves before continuing. 'I think we should turn all the diagnosis pods off. We don't have the necessary drugs to treat every little complaint and we can't cope with hysterical patients demanding treatment for conditions that only have the potential to manifest. It's a waste of what limited resources we do have left.'

'I agree,' said Jed. 'Force has been stretched thin keeping the peace...'

He was interrupted by Sean. 'Surely the Security Guards can help monitor the situation?' He inclined his head at Jed.

'Let's hope so, but we can do without unnecessary disturbances at Medical,' snapped Jed.

'How will you switch off the diagnostic pods without access to the Corporation mainframe?' Ruth narrowed her eyes suspiciously at Dr Lee.

'We have the kill code for the pods. One of the Med-

Techs kept scrupulous records, surprisingly this is one code that still works. We tested it in the outlying pods in East Sector.'

Martha nodded. 'Okay, do it. Terminate the diagnostic pods. I'll send out a sweep informing citizens that we're diverting resources elsewhere, hopefully it won't cause too much panic.'

'It should help, but it doesn't solve our main problem,' replied Dr Lee.

'I know but...' Martha was interrupted.

'I'm sorry Ma'am, but I don't think you do. Without a resupply in the next week or so, citizens will potentially start falling ill and I won't be able to do anything about it. Then we will have mass panic to deal with.' Dr Lee looked around the room. 'We've got to do something.'

'Did City 15 respond to any of our communiques yet, Jed?' Martha asked.

'No, we've had nothing back. Agent Devereaux hasn't reported back yet either. We've had no confirmation that the original messages have even got through to them.'

'I think we have to send a full exploration team out there. Not just an emissary from our city but some scientists and an archivist as well, plus security of course.' Martha felt a flicker of worry. She didn't care for Devereaux very much, but she certainly didn't want anything to happen to him, especially when he was meant to be on a fact-finding mission for her government.

'That would be my recommendation as well,' Jed said. 'We don't even know if Devereaux got to City 15 safely, one man travelling on his own... anything could've happened.' He opened a file on his handheld and sent it to the main screen to display the map from

City 42 to City 15 to the others. 'If you look at the terrain, we'd have to cross a dead zone but overall it's not far. We know the transporters aren't working between the cities so it could be that the people of 15 are wondering what's happening over here. We might even run into an envoy from them as we head out over there.'

'Do we have the means to get a full exploration team out there?' asked Martha.

Jed nodded. 'We've got the Force skimmers; they'll do the journey alright. I've got a few people in mind for the team. If it's alright with you, we'll leave tomorrow.' He felt excited, this would be his first mission as Captain and although it was concerning that Devereaux had gone incommunicado, he didn't think anything would've happened to the man. He was too annoying to go missing.

'Make sure you're fully prepared for every scenario, Jed. You will need a diplomatic envoy as well as Force operatives. I do think you should take an archivist and scientists as well as a security force. We don't even know whether 15 will let you in. After all they're still Corporation and we're not,' said Martha.

'I don't think that will be much of a problem,' Ruth observed. 'City 15 has always had strong Anti-Corp roots. It's where the first revolution happened.'

'And failed,' muttered Sean under his breath.

'Well, be careful, please.' Martha's headache was receding somewhat but the churning whirlpool of worry in her stomach more than made up for the lack of pounding. 'I don't want anything to happen to anyone. Could you leave the details of your team with me, please Jed?'-

'Will do.'

'What's next on the agenda, Sean?' asked Martha.

'Citizens have been expressing their unease again at the lack of a force-field. There's been a lot of chatter on the sweeps about letting in disease and vermin although of course those are only rumours. We've had no such actual reports.' Sean looked up from his handheld. 'The new security teams seem to be going down well.'

'Good, well done Sean. That was a great idea, to have the public responsible for their own safety gets everyone more invested in the city. If no-one has any objections, I'll get the updates office to re-sweep the batch of notices we used last month, the ones about the safety beyond the city walls.' Martha looked down the table but there were no objections, so she made a note to action that point. It was something Sean could do but Martha liked to keep her hand in with the day-to-day when she could. 'I also think it's time to roll out a new campaign to encourage citizens to try the fresh food that is coming in from Camp Eden - can you put together some sweeps please, Sean?'

Sean nodded and made a note. 'Food sachets are running low as well, Governor Hamble. We do need to come up with a more permanent solution. Perhaps if we reached out to City 9?'

Jed's ears perked up. 'I think we should wait until we've been to City 15 before we go any further afield,' he said. 'They are likely to be a bit more receptive than a Corporation stronghold.'

Sean smiled and shrugged.

'I quite agree, Jed. One step at a time.' Martha glanced outside at the view overlooking Main Square below. She smiled at the bee that bumped into the window before her attention was distracted by the small crowd gathering at the base of the building. 'As you all probably noticed there is a peaceful protest happening this afternoon in the square. I believe it's another demonstration against the closure of the baby labs but let me assure all of you, that decision is final and will not be revoked.'

'But Governor, all the people want is to raise a family. Like you.' Sean looked a picture of innocence. He had been pushing Martha for weeks to re-open the labs. 'Surely you don't want riots like we had when citizens found out about the baby sales?'

'We did not have riots. The people reacted emotionally to a shocking situation and I will not blame them for that. But my decision is final. Those labs are not opening again until we find out where all the documented babies grown disappeared to, because they certainly aren't here in City 42.' Martha's nostrils were flaring as she tried to keep her anger under control. She had been absolutely horrified to learn that extra babies had been grown out of their reproduction labs. She was more disturbed that they were unable to find out where the babies had been sent thanks to the computer shutdowns. It was something she was desperate to find out. Martha sounded firm yet her brow was creased with worry. 'Dr Lee, do you know why we haven't had more natural pregnancies?'

The Surgeon General huffed a little before answering. 'As we said before, it will take time for each individual reproductive system to recover from the illegal radiation we all experienced. Everyone will be different, it could take months, it could take generations. We have had some miscarriages which, whilst they are sad news for the couples involved, are encouraging. It shows our natural systems are gradually getting back to normal.'

'Is there anything more we can tell the public?' asked

Sean.

'Not really, but we can re-sweep our previous messages, if you think that will help.' Dr Lee looked to Martha, rather than Sean and she nodded in agreement before turning her attention to the next item, education.

Professor Kamir had chosen to step down from his position as Head of Academy and consequently his place on Martha's ruling committee. Ruth had been put forward as liaison due to her teaching background and it was agreed by everyone present that she was an excellent replacement, but Martha wasn't sure whether Ruth was coping well with the new role and motherhood. It was tough on both of them.

'Ruth, how are things at Academy?'

But Ruth didn't answer. She was staring off into space, her head cocked as if she were listening to something else. There was a bee crawling around the window frame closest to her. Martha had to say Ruth's name three times before she realised everyone was looking at her, waiting for her to speak.

'Academy. Right.' Ruth tapped her handheld a few times then read out her report woodenly. 'New curriculum implemented. Lots of interest on the new courses, less actual uptake. Postgraduates are filling in staff gaps where possible. Attendance is still good.' She looked up to see whether she could get away with that recap.

There were no objections to the report, so Ruth moved on to the other update she had available. 'Archive has been busy. They are ensuring all citizens have access to relevant information, but all terrorist related items are strictly monitored and still require governor approval before they can be accessed.'

Sean coughed and Martha looked at him. 'Did you

have anything to add to the report, Sean?'

'No, no, you go ahead Ma'am.'

'Right, well, I think that's everything on the agenda. Any other business?' Martha cleared her handheld screen, hoping to be able to make a quick getaway for once.

'Um, I have a couple of items - if it's alright?' Sean asked.

'Of course.' Martha concealed her surprise, she thought Sean had raised everything with her in the short briefing they'd had before this meeting.

'There has been a significant social backlash on the issue of Corp Tech.' Jed looked up sharply and Sean raised his hands in defence. 'It's not coming from me. This is actual chatter. I can show you the screen grabs if you like.' He went to activate the main screen in the room, but Martha forestalled him.

'That's not necessary, Sean. I know many citizens feel we should reopen Corp Tech and continue working on the projects we have been able to recover but until we can solve the supplies issue I think we should be focusing on making sure everyone has enough to eat and any medical needs are met.

'But I think...'

'No, Sean. Now is not the time.' Martha's voice came out sharper than she intended making Ruth flinch slightly. She took a calming breath. 'Anything else?'

Sean had reddened at the admonition but still had one more point he wanted to raise. 'The er... matter of the worshippers. They are starting to become a social nuisance. The new security teams have informed me...'

This time it was Jed who interrupted. 'Do you mean the Gaia followers? How are they a social nuisance?'

Sean bristled. 'Well, they insist on communing with

30

nature right out in the open, causing obstructions in public places and there has been effigy.'

Ruth barked a laugh. 'You can't stop people from meeting in public places - they are public, they have every right to meet.'

'Yes but...'

'No, Sean. Ruth is right. If citizens want to meet in public spaces and celebrate nature, I for one am certainly not going to stop them. As for the effigy, leave it. It's a symbol of hope for many people. Art should be treasured, not destroyed.'

'But they're planting flowers? Encouraging bees!' Sean protested.

'And that is a good thing, Sean. Trust me,' replied Martha.

Sean twisted his mouth slightly as he reluctantly nodded and put his handheld down.

There was a moment of silence. Jed stood up to leave. 'We done?'

'I think so, Jed. Can you wait in my office though please? I'd like to sign off on your guard selection and approve all your supplies.'

Jed nodded and the Surgeon General scooped up his papers in relief. Martha turned her attention to him. 'Treat the essentials, as best you can,' she said. Dr Lee nodded and left the room with Jed close on his heels. Sean bustled out shortly afterwards.

The two women left looked at each other, mirroring their exhaustion.

'Are we done for the day?' Ruth asked hopefully.

'Nearly. You head home. I'll see you there, I want to sign off on Jed's expedition team. I want to make sure he has decent medical and scientific support as well as brute force. Plus, there's the Archivist position to fill - do you think Kira would go?'

Ruth screwed up her face, frowning. 'I don't think she'd leave Grace behind.'

'No, you're right. But if this really is a diplomatic mission then there will be plenty of security and there's no reason to think they wouldn't be safe. It's only City 15.'

'Alright, well you'll have to ask her and see what she thinks. Try not to get caught up in anything else. You look tired.'

'Thanks, I thought I'd try and give you some competition.' The two friends smiled at each other wearily before leaving the conference room together. One to head home to worry about the children, the other to worry some more about all the citizens who relied on her to keep them safe.

GOVHAM: *Our monthly meeting report is available to download. Together we're looking after City 42.*

ANON17: *How does shutting down diagnostic pods help look after us? It's a conspiracy! Killing off the undesirable!*

MED4C42: *Diagnostic pods will be temporarily offline. If you have any serious health concerns, visit your nearest med centre.*

GOVHAM: *Re-sharing our Safety Beyond the Wall info jack. Download yours today and discover the wonders outside. Together we're looking after City 42.*

ANON17: *Don't believe a word - it's a toxic wasteland! Bring back the force-field! Bring back the force-field!*

MSCHILD: *Maybe no force-field is the reason why no pregnancies? Open the baby labs! It's not fair.*

MED4C42: *Find out more about the natural pregnancy cycle. Download your info jack & get up to speed. You could be next!*

ANON17: *Rehashing - resharing - same old, same old. Lies, lies, lies, lies!*

CAMPEDEN: *Visit our online tour today. Discover how the hydroponics centre is growing fresh food for you & your family. It's safe - it's healthy - it's delicious!*

ANON40: *I'd rather eat a dry sachet.*

ENCRYPTED MESSAGE FROM 7421 TO NEW CORP

>>1. The new Corp Tech supporters' group is gaining momentum. Previous employees are desperate to start working on the latest tech. Can I leak the new neural implants yet?

2. Shall I have the appointment of Jed Jenkins to Captain of the City Guard invalidated?

3. They've decided to turn off the medical diagnostic pods. Will you be bringing medical supplies? Things are running low.

4. There is continual backlash about the force-field remaining switched off. I have made sure that all the equipment remains intact.

5. You gave me no instructions for City 15 - they are sending another team out there<<

ENCRYPTED MESSAGE FROM CORP TO 7421
>>REPORT RECEIVED.

1. CONTINUE TO SUPPORT THE CORP TECH MOVEMENT. DO NOT LEAK THE NEURAL IMPLANTS YET. WE WILL BRING IT WITH US.

2. CHIEF MINKOV WILL BE DEALT WITH. DO NOTHING TO JEOPARDISE YOUR POSITION. IF JENKINS LEAVES THE CITY, WE WILL DEAL WITH HIM.

3. SUPPLIES WILL BE PROVIDED FOR THOSE LOYAL TO NEW CORP.

4. CONTINUE TO PROTECT THE FORCE-FIELD EQUIPMENT. WE WILL BE SWITCHING IT BACK ON.

5. PLANS FOR CITY 15 ARE IN MOTION.

STAND BY FOR FURTHER INSTRUCTIONS<<

Chapter 4

'Who are you taking with you?' asked Kira as she sat with her husband while he gathered his gear together. She was smiling as she watched him, he seemed more like himself since getting the promotion and the mission. Ever since Pete's death, Jed had been more short-tempered. He'd had fights at Force over imagined slurs, refused to work with anyone else and had become withdrawn. He wasn't sharing things with her anymore. She understood it was part of his coping mechanism, but it sometimes made her feel like a stranger in her own marriage.

'Oh, you know, some of the lads from Force - Ash, you've met him. And there will be a couple of others.'

Kira waited for him to elaborate but he didn't. 'Um,

35

won't there be some sort of scientist and medical presence as well? Isn't it a diplomatic mission?'

'Martha wants me to take Max so I was going to speak to him next. Don't worry about the medical though love, we're all trained in first aid. We'll have med kits with us.' He continued stuffing clothes into a bag.

There was a short silence, broken only by Grace's happy babbling from the front room. Kira wrung her hands together, trying to find the right words. She couldn't bring herself to tell him about her involvement, so she changed tack.

'You will, I mean, it's not dangerous is it? You're going to be alright?'

Jed stopped packing and looked at his wife. His heart ached, he loved her so much, but he felt like he couldn't tell her. Things were still so raw and emotional for him. He honestly believed that if he let in his love for Kira then his grief for his sister and Pete would overwhelm him, and right now he needed to keep functioning. One step at a time.

'We are only going to City 15. We'll be fine. There's obviously been some sort of mix-up on the access codes or something, which is why we can't talk to the city anymore.' He turned his attention back to packing.

'But why have they stopped sending their skimmers over? Do you think they will try to attack us?' She winced hoping he hadn't noticed exactly what she'd said.

'I hardly think that's likely, love.' Jed zipped up his bag. 'City 15 have never been staunchly Corporation. I bet they've followed our lead and got rid of their board of directors. They've probably been locked out of their main systems, like we were.'

'You really think that?' Kira was doubtful.

'I'm sure. Everything is going to be fine. I've got to

chat to Max over at Eden now. Alright if I use the main vid?' Kira nodded. Jed picked up his bag and left the bedroom, but Kira couldn't get rid of the sinking feeling in the pit of her stomach.

It took a few minutes for the connection to Camp Eden to clear. There was a lot of static on the vid feed and broken sound until finally it resolved into a clear image.

'Hi Jed, sorry about that. We had a loose wire, looks alright our end now.' Max plonked himself down into a camping chair, looking as tanned and laid-back as ever.

'Yep, reading you loud and clear here as well,' Jed replied.

'So, what's going on, how can I help?'

'Yeah, sorry it's not a social call. We, the governor's office I mean, are putting together an expedition to go over to City 15 and I'd like you, and Dina, to come with us,' Jed explained.

'Really? Why do you want us?' Max beckoned to someone off cam and Dina's face appeared.

'Hi Jed! How are you? How's Kira and Grace?'

Jed grinned at Dina's infectious cheerfulness. 'Hi D. We're all fine, but as I was saying, we want you and Max to come on an expedition to City 15 with us.'

'Oh exciting! Are we going?' Dina looked at Max who nodded.

'I guess we are. But, Jed, you still haven't told me why you want us along?'

'Well, we've had no luck making contact with City 15 since Corporation left 42. And we're running low on medical and food supplies, as you know. Governor Hamble wants us to reach out to 15 personally and find out how we can build a working relationship with them. Having you guys there will help us explain what

37

happened with the water supply and the new food we're growing at Camp. Plus...' Jed trailed off and looked to make sure Kira was still occupied and hadn't come into the room. He hunched closer to the vid screen and lowered his voice. 'We haven't had any response, to any of our communiques. And a previous envoy has gone missing. I think there might be something seriously wrong.'

'What do you mean?' Dina frowned. 'Do you think Corp have done something?'

'I don't know. But it's a possibility.'

Max broke the silence. 'Okay Jed, we'll come and help, of course we will. When do you need us?'

'Appreciate it, Max. Tomorrow. I need you at City 42, first thing tomorrow and...' Dina cut across him.

'What do you mean *first thing tomorrow*! We're doing important work here at Eden. We can't drop everything at a moment's notice to travel to a city where they may or may not want to talk to us.' Dina's cheeks were flushed as she finished speaking.

'Easy, Dina. Jed, of course. We'll be at Main Square for 9am don't worry.' Max put a placating hand on Dina's shoulders and shook his head slightly as she opened her mouth to complain some more.

'Thanks, Max. Appreciate it. See you tomorrow.' Jed signed off the vid comm. He was glad he wasn't in Max's shoes right now. He didn't actually need Dina on the team, but Jed would never have got away with only recruiting Max for the mission. If he'd had his way, he wouldn't have recruited any civilians. Much better to only have his operatives and scope out the situation with them. Jed checked over his bag, one more time, to make sure he had everything he needed. Tomorrow was going to be an interesting day.

Kira listened to make sure Jed was still busy and unlikely to disturb her before she vid-commed her mum.

'Kira, honey, how are you my dear? I was just saying to your father we hadn't heard from you today. You sure you're eating enough, love? You look a bit peaky. It's all well and good eating that newfangled earth grown stuff but you ought to get a couple of sachets as well. It's not natural to rely on the real food alone. I was telling Maureen the other day - she's convinced that we'll be running out of sachets soon and everyone will be reduced to eating beetles and bugs.' Jean Bishop laughed loudly. 'Can you imagine? Beetles and bugs!'

'Mum!' Kira cut in urgently. 'Mum, listen, I can't talk for long. But...' She cocked her head to make sure Jed wasn't coming into the bedroom. 'I'm going to City 15 and I'm taking Grace with me.' *And I haven't told Jed yet* she thought to herself.

'Oh, that'll be nice, dear.'

Kira frowned. 'Did you hear what I said?'

'I may be your mother but I'm not past it yet, dear. You said you were going to City 15 and taking Grace with you. Visiting friends are you, love?'

'Er, no Mum. Martha's asked me to go as an Archive advisor. It's part of a diplomatic mission.' Kira scratched her head. 'You do know that we haven't had any contact from 15 for weeks, don't you, Mum?'

'Oh, I'm sure it's a switched off button somewhere, love. It's all a bit above my head. But a trip will do you good. Get some colour in those cheeks, all that fresh air.' Suddenly Jean seemed to realise that City 15 was a fair distance away from City 42 and involved travelling through the countryside that may or may not be safe. 'But you will have protection, won't you? And you're taking Grace? Are you sure that's a good idea, love? I

39

know it's important to you to raise the child as naturally as possible but exposing her to potentially lethal toxins might be taking it a step too far. Although it is important for her to have new experiences that's true. Is Jed going with you? Of course he is, he wouldn't let you go running off on some mad scheme without him. He'll be there to protect and look after you, keep you out of trouble. Aww it'll be nice, a family trip out. Only do watch out for those animals. I hear all sorts of stories about real animals lurking outside the city walls. Waiting around, looking for any excuse to come in and eat us all in our beds. Why I was telling Jackie the other day...'

Kira let her mother's incessant chatter flow over her. It felt normal and safe and calmed her down. She was nervous about going on this mission, but she had argued her case to Martha intelligently. They did need someone with Archival clearance and a working knowledge of City 15 plus she didn't feel comfortable letting Jed go away without her. And anyway, Kira would make sure absolutely nothing bad happened to her daughter.

Chapter 5

GOVHAM: Join me in wishing our first inter-city mission success. Together we're looking after City 42.

ANON17: Together we're wasting resources.

C42N: Will City 15 open trade routes with an independent city? What do you think? Join the discussion in social hub beta.

Martha groaned as her alarm blared. At least it wasn't a baby crying. Then Lucas started wailing. So much for that. She pushed herself to sitting and blinked blearily. Lucas was still asleep in his cube. Must be Sarah crying, poor Ruth. Come to think of it, poor Martha! She crept out of the bedroom, trying not to wake her son and went to put on the synth-caf and bottle warmers. Lucas might not be awake right now, but it wouldn't be long.

Ruth stumbled into the kitchen with Sarah in arms.

'Oh, thank you,' she said as she saw the warmer already on. 'I can't seem to get going this morning. Sorry about the wake-up call.'

Martha smiled. 'It's fine - we've got a big day, might as well start getting ready for it.'

'You finalised the team, then?' Ruth fumbled with the bottle nearly dropping both it and her baby. Martha's quicker reflexes stopped the bottle from falling off the counter. 'Thanks, sorry. Again.' Ruth was flustered.

'Are you alright, Ruth?' Martha touched her friend's arm in concern. 'Why don't you drop the kids in at the office crèche, get some rest - you've more than earned it. I can look in on them.'

'No, it's alright. I can manage.' She forced a smile. 'I'm fine, honestly. I've never been at my best first thing in the morning. Ah, I think that's your noise-bag.'

New cries filled the air as Lucas made it clear that he was awake and would like his breakfast. Now. Martha hurried back to her room to scoop up her son and returned, chatting to him. 'Morning angel-face, let's get you sorted out. Come on, come on, here it is. There, there. It's alright.'

The kitchen was filled with the sound of two contented babies as their mums leant against worktops and considered the day ahead.

'Jed's not going to be happy about this, you know.' Ruth commented finally.

'No, he's not. But she's right, he can be reckless, and we don't need that on a fact-finding mission. At least this way he won't take unnecessary risks.'

'You hope.'

Martha sighed. 'We need to find out what's happening in City 15. We've got to get these supply routes back open. And we need to start talking to Corporation, one way or another.'

Ruth snorted. She didn't agree with that last part. Now that they were free of Corp, she didn't think they should be so quick to extend an olive branch, but Martha felt they could come to some sort of agreement. 'I still

42

think you're making a mistake. If you invite Corp in, they will take over again and who knows what they'll do to you. Don't you think it sends a mixed message kicking them out only to invite them back for synth-caf?'

'It's not that straightforward and you know it, Ruth. We have to get the medical supply chain restarted, it's crucial, but I'm not going to let them lie to us again.'

There was a strained silence between the two women.

'Right, I think these guys have finished. Are you coming with me to see the exploration team off?' Martha asked.

Ruth nodded and rushed to get her bag organised. Martha smiled at her friend, she seemed fine. Kira had pinged her to say she was worried about Ruth, but she seemed the same as always to Martha. Having someone else struggling with being a single parent while working was a blessing. At least she had someone to talk about it with. Setting up the crèche facilities at Hamble HQ for when both of them had to work had been relatively easy but it didn't stop Martha from feeling guilty, like she was letting Lucas down every time she left him there to go to work. But she was governor. She, if nobody else, had to put the citizens of City 42 first.

'You don't have to come with me, you know. We can say goodbye here.' Jed was impatient to leave. The expedition team were meeting up and heading out to City 15 this morning. It felt good to have something proactive to get on with, away from all the memories City 42 held.

'I know, but we are. You ready?' Kira had Grace all bundled up, looking like they were about to begin an expedition instead of Jed. He noticed that their skimmer was also full of bags.

'Are you planning to stay with your mum for a few days, then?' Jed asked.

Kira murmured noncommittally as she buckled Grace into her safety seat and then began piloting the skimmer towards Hamble HQ. Jed looked out the window at the city buildings. Martha taking over Collection Towers for her government offices was working well, so far. The rubble from the destruction of Corp Tech had been cleared but nothing new had been decided on yet. *It will probably end up as a memorial space* Jed reflected. A fitting tribute.

It didn't take long to get to Hamble HQ. It looked like everyone else on the team was already assembled. Even Ruth was there. Jed scrambled out of the skimmer, grabbing his gear on his way, leaving Kira to deal with Grace.

Martha smiled nervously at him as he came over. 'Morning, Jed. Are you ready?'

Jed nodded, eager to get the formalities over with so they could be on their way. His team were already packed into a couple of Force skimmers and Ash discreetly took Jed's gear away, stowing it securely in one of their vehicles.

'I believe you know the science team.' Martha was grinning as both Max and Dina came forward from the small crowd now gathering.

'Good to see you, buddy,' Jed clasped hands with Max firmly and smiled genuinely at him. When Dina had decided to stay out at Camp Eden with Max, initially the group had worried about her, but Max had been there for her and together, their relationship had blossomed. It was good to see them both again. 'I'm not sure there'll be much scientific for you guys to get stuck into but happy to have you on board. Hey, D.'

Dina hugged him. 'You never know what we might find out there, that's the best bit!' She was excited and looked past Jed to wave enthusiastically at Kira and Grace.

'I still think you should take a Med Tech with you.' Martha put up a hand to forestall Jed's arguments for not taking one. 'I know, I know, all the guys from Force have basic first aid but we don't know what we're walking into and I wanted you to have someone who knows intimately what supplies we need urgently.'

'You've given us the list. I'm sure we can figure it out. We've got Max and Dina with us for any science jargon. It'll be fine. We're going to City 15, not the back end of beyond.' Jed didn't want any more civilians on this mission, just in case.

'Hmm.' Martha didn't sound convinced, but she had already given in to Jed's request for no more civilians yesterday when she'd mentioned a med-tech. She knew he wasn't going to like what she had to tell him next. 'As I said yesterday, I want you to take someone from Archive, to document the journey and to gather any pertinent information from City 15 while you're there. I believe you know each other.' Martha waited anxiously for Jed to connect the dots.

He looked, lips pressed into a thin line, eyes narrowed from Martha to Kira who had come to join them. 'I suppose this was all your idea?' he asked his wife. She shrugged self-consciously, aware of everyone else's gaze upon them. 'What about Grace?'

'She's coming as well,' replied Kira.

'What? Do you think that's a sensible idea?'

'I do.' Kira decided against saying anything else with

everyone watching, they could discuss it later. She and Martha had talked about it at length last night. They both hoped having his family along would ground Jed somewhat and prevent too much reckless behaviour. And besides, the expedition did need an archivist.

Jed stared at his wife, he was irritated that she went behind his back, but he knew he couldn't show it now, in front of the entire expedition. He was also annoyed to admit to himself that Kira was the most qualified archivist they had so it made sense to bring her along, even though he'd prefer someone else. She had been studying everything Archive held on the other nearby cities, and without full access to their own systems as they travelled, it could be invaluable information. He nodded curtly and waited to see if there were to be any further surprises.

Martha let out a breath she hadn't realised she'd been holding. She turned and addressed the small crowd in front of her.

'I want to thank you all for volunteering for this mission to City 15. We don't know what you will find when you get there but I am confident you have the skills and experience to deal with any situation. Remember, we want to establish a line of communication and more importantly, supply routes.' She paused to look at the people in front of her. 'Corporation are not the enemy.'

There was a lot of muttering and side wise glances from the members of the expedition team. Martha held up her hand.

'Please, let me finish. I'm not saying Corporation are blameless, but the fact of the matter is, we simply do not know their level of influence in other cities. We cannot assume the same blanket control throughout, we must go forward with an open mind and gather all the facts. I look to all of you to be our fact gatherers, our champions and our protectors.'

There was a smattering of applause. Most of the team were serious and resolute, keen to begin their mission. Martha looked at her friends, Kira and Dina were smiling at her at least, Ruth seemed pensive. Martha walked towards them, trying to ignore the knot of worry in her stomach.

'Great speech,' Dina teased.

'You will both be extra careful, won't you?' Martha asked. 'Especially you, Kira. No risk taking. Keep Grace safe.'

'I will.' Kira was feeling nervous now, it had seemed like such a good idea at the time. Was she making a mistake? Was bringing Grace along the most dangerous thing she could do?

The women hugged, eyes glinting yet smiling at each other. Jed whistled to get everyone's attention. His team were ready to leave, all kit stowed and everyone within the vehicles. Kira, Dina and Max hurried to the second skimmer. Once Grace was safely ensconced inside, Kira had a brief panic that she hadn't thought of everything but reminded herself that it was unlikely she'd forgotten anything significant. Being a mother had forced her to be organised, whether she was naturally inclined to be so or not.

Martha watched the skimmers leave the plaza in single file. She hoped she wasn't making a mistake. Ruth came to stand next to her. A bee bumbled along nearby, unnoticed by either of them. Both women too preoccupied with their own thoughts and worries.

'Everything go okay?'

'I think so. Jed took it well, I thought.' Martha tried

to sound positive.

'Yeah? Well, I wouldn't like to be in Kira's shoes later.' Ruth linked arms with Martha and the two women started walking away.

'She can hold her own, believe me. Jed will probably come away thinking it was all part of his great idea in the first place.'

Ruth chuckled but like Martha, she couldn't quite shake the feeling of impending doom. Their friends were travelling into the unknown, all they could do now was wait.

Chapter 6

At first the journey was exciting. The small convoy passed close by Max's science base; Camp Eden. Both he and Dina kept Kira amused with anecdotes about their life in the camp and pointed out the interesting flora and fauna as they passed. But soon the vehicles travelled into a burn zone, where nature had yet to conquer the radioactive ravages inflicted upon the planet by man. It was a sobering contrast to the lush young forests that surrounded Camp Eden.

'Do we know why this land hasn't recovered yet, Max?' Kira asked.

'The soil is too acidic. We know there were heavier HER attacks in certain places but without the remains of any landmarks it's difficult to know what was here before. It could've been a military base or a government building of some kind.'

'Will the ground ever recover?'

'It should do, in time,' Max replied. 'All we can do is hope that with enough care and attention, Mother Nature will spread her magic a little further for us.'

'You mean Gaia.' Kira smiled at the sun-kissed scientist.

'Yes, our fabulous blue lady.'

'Any more sightings?' Kira hadn't seen or felt Gaia since the events leading up to the overthrow of Corporation and the beginning of the new governance under Martha's leadership.

'No,' Dina replied sadly. 'Sometimes I wonder whether we imagined it all in the first place but then I remind myself of the recording we have and all our individual experiences. I know she's real but, I suppose she has more important things to do at the moment then come and see us. There have been bee sightings inside the city though, that's exciting.'

'I know, we saw one the other day. There's also a small collection of Gaia followers who have been terrorising Sean,' replied Kira.

'Sean? Isn't he Martha's aide?' asked Max.

'Yeah, that's him.'

'What sort of things have they been doing?' asked Dina, she was intrigued.

Kira laughed. 'Oh, highly inflammatory stuff like meeting in the new parks, planting flowers and I think one of them painted a picture of Gaia on a blank wall.'

'Oh,' Dina sounded disappointed for a moment. 'Was it a good picture?'

'It didn't look much like Her. I don't think they've seen the real thing, like us.' Kira paused, feeling saddened that there hadn't been any new sightings. 'You never know, City 15 might have some blue lady tales for us.'

'Do you think Corporation is still in charge over there?' Dina was doubtful. She was from City 15 originally and although she only had scattered memories of her childhood there, she knew the reason she'd been orphaned and left the city was down to Anti-Corp uprisings.

'I honestly don't know. I'm just hoping we can reconnect the medical supply train.' Kira hadn't told her friends yet but, her Mum needed regular medicine to keep a mutated genetic condition under control. With the disrupted supply chains, the medicine Jean Bishop needed was dwindling fast, despite Kira and her family's efforts to stockpile as much as possible. With no new supplies arriving, they would run out soon and then Kira's mum would swiftly begin to deteriorate and become severely ill. And Kira knew her mum would not be the only one. The reduced medical supplies were a taboo subject as everyone tried to manage their own needs privately. There wasn't much of a community sharing spirit when it came to such a serious situation. Kira couldn't blame them; people were trying to keep their families safe. That was the reason for this expedition after all.

Chapter 7

City 15 was smaller than 42 but laid out in a similar grid pattern. There was a greater Academy presence here; it had been originally designed to be a city of learning. Its Professors would often visit 42 for guest lectures but no-one had been for months, not since City 42 overthrew Corporation.

As the envoy approached, Ash swept the city for its protective force-field.

'Huh.'

'What?' Jed looked at the screen on the dashboard.

'There's no force-field.'

'On alert people.' Jed called back to the rest of his team. 'We don't know what we're going into.' Jed pressed the comm channel to speak to the other transporter. 'Kira? Pick up please.'

'Yes, Jed? We're here.'

'The city force-field is down so we're going in on high alert. I want you to stay inside your vehicle at all times. It's armoured for your protection.'

'Uh... okay.' Kira looked at her fellow passengers in alarm, but Max and Dina seemed relaxed about the news and smiled reassuringly so she tried to push her unease away.

Jed watched the dashboard as Ash ran through all the usual checks. There was no response to their hails. The force-field was down. Comms were unresponsive. Power signatures were negative. It looked like there was no-one there at all.

The two vehicles passed through the open gateway and followed the empty road towards the middle of the city. There were no skimmers, no lights, no people. No signs of life at all.

'Where is everyone?' murmured Ash. Every building scan was coming up empty.

'If we knew that, we wouldn't be here.' Jed felt like they were walking straight into a trap and he'd brought his wife and child along for the ride. He glanced back through the rear-view to reassure himself the second vehicle was still there. It was.

They arrived at the central plaza. Still devoid of life. Jed gave out the orders.

'Alpha Team, I want you to use your rebreathers and fan out. Do a block-by-block check, out to ten blocks then report back. Scan the buildings but don't enter them. Report in if you see anything suspicious. Stay together.'

There were confident assurances from the team. The operatives were used to working together and the four of them left the skimmer eagerly to explore what was happening in City 15.

'Ash, run a diagnostic on what is working here. There has to be some sort of signal somewhere. The rest of Beta Team, with me.' Jed left the skimmer, confident that Ash would check everything that could be checked. He was a solid team member; you could always count on his level-headedness in a crisis.

When Jed got to the second skimmer, Kira popped out to see him straight away.

'I thought I told you to stay in the vehicle at all times.'

'Jed! What's going on? Where is everyone?'

'I don't know, love. We're running scans and checking what we can. I need you to stay here and stay safe, okay?' He kissed her on the cheek then beckoned to Max to move within speaking range.

'Max. I need you and Dina to run some air quality tests. I don't know why we haven't met anyone yet, but just in case I want to make sure the atmosphere isn't toxic.'

'Of course. We'll go find a water sample as well. Best to be on the safe side.'

'Do you have your rebreathers with you?' Jed asked.

'Yeah,' Max fumbled in his bag and drew out a pair. Kira looked on, wide eyed as Dina and Max put on the rebreathers and left the skimmer to begin running their tests.

'I don't have a rebreather, neither does Grace,' she told her husband in a small voice.

'Which is why you are staying in the vehicle.' Jed gave her a quick kiss and pushed her gently back into the skimmer. 'Let us run these initial tests. Make sure everything is safe before you come out.' He closed the skimmer door, leaving Kira to stare after him as he put on his rebreather and led Beta Team across the opposite side of the plaza to start scanning the buildings in that direction.

'Well, I guess that leaves us on our own then, Gracie.' Kira spoke aloud but the little girl didn't stir, the skimmer journey having lulled her to sleep. All Kira could do was watch the two teams of City Guard operatives venture out into the city and her friends standing in the middle of the plaza, scanning the air quality. It didn't take that long before Max took off his rebreather and gave Kira a thumbs up signal. She sighed. She probably ought to stay in the skimmer. Frag it. Grace was fast asleep, and it wasn't like she was going to go far. She carefully opened the door, closed it behind her and escaped into the plaza.

'Air's alright then?' Kira smiled up at Max.

'Yep. Nothing going on that I can tell. There's no insect life though, which is peculiar. We'd expect to register something at least.' He tapped his handheld a few times. 'We need to find a water supply now - any ideas, Kira? You've been to City 15 before, haven't you?'

Kira shook her head. 'No, but I did some research on the city before we left. If this is Central Plaza, then...' She spun round and pointed at a large, imposing building behind them with what looked like marble columns around huge wooden doors. 'That is the Academy Library - there will be a public water supply in there. Let me get Grace and I'll come with you.'

Dina frowned. 'Didn't Jed tell you to stay in the skimmer?'

Kira stared at Dina until she laughed self-consciously and raised her hands in defeat. Kira stalked away. She wasn't some fragile touchscreen; she was more than capable of looking after herself and her child. When she got back to the skimmer, Grace was beginning to stir. By the time Kira had checked her nappy and gathered together all the paraphernalia she needed to take with her, Max and Dina were standing outside, bored expressions on their faces. Kira felt even more irritated. People without children had no idea how long it took to do the simplest of things. Securing Grace into her carrier, Kira slammed the skimmer door shut and began walking towards the Academy Library. Max and

Dina scrambled to catch up with her.

'Got everything?' Max asked.

'Yep.'

He took longer strides in order to get in front of Kira. 'I think I ought to go into the building first, you know. Just in case.'

Kira was still feeling annoyed, but she knew he was right. She didn't want to walk headfirst into danger and she certainly didn't want to put Grace in harm's way. Dina linked her arm through Kira's and smiled tentatively. Kira relaxed; she was overreacting. She squeezed arms with Dina and looked ahead to see what the library had to offer.

It was impressive. As Max swung the doors open, the interior gleamed in the light. Obviously, the library wasn't full of actual books, they were kept safe in Archive but, there were rows and rows of info booths with mounted screens and a variety of seating options from percher stools to full on recliners so students could browse the extensive cache of information in comfort. Max swept the general area with his handheld and turned back to the others.

'There doesn't seem to be anything wrong with the atmosphere. No heat signatures either. There's no-one here.'

'No-one?' Dina was surprised. She thought the citizens would've come here for safety from whatever had happened in City 15.

Kira walked over to the nearest touchscreen and tried to activate it. Nothing. The screen remained blank. 'Looks like there's no power here, either. Dead.'

They all jumped as the door banged behind them and Jed strode in with the rest of Beta Team. They took their rebreathers off when they saw the others weren't wearing them.

'I thought I told you to stay in the vehicle?' He ran an anxious glance over Kira and Grace.

'We're fine. Max checked the atmosphere, it's all clear here. No toxins. No people either, apparently.' Kira swept an arm over the interior of the library and pointed to the touchscreens. 'All dead.'

Jed nodded. 'We've found nothing either. All building sweeps are coming up empty. I'm waiting for Alpha Team to check in and then I'll report to Martha.'

Max cleared his throat. 'What's our next step here then?'

'Well, we'll release a couple of drones to do a more thorough sweep of the city, in case our initial once over missed anything. I'll program one to do the perimeter as well, see what we can find. It's up to Governor Hamble what we do after that.'

'Right.' Max nodded thoughtfully but whatever he was going to say was interrupted by the return of Alpha Team.

'Nothing to report, Sir,' said the Alpha Team leader.

'Right, let's head back to the skimmers and set up a makeshift camp. I want a perimeter with lookouts. We still don't know what happened here,' Jed said.

The City Guard operatives nodded and moved with purpose back to their skimmer to unpack the equipment and sleeping pods. Max, Dina and Kira trailed behind. This wasn't turning out to be quite the field trip they had expected.

'Ash, anything to report?' Jed poked his head into the front of the skimmer with the comms system.

'It's not good, Sir. The city mainframe has been locked out, just like ours, so there's no way of communicating with 42 or accessing 15's supply

57

manifest. The best I can do is tell you where their Med Centre is then we can go and see if there's anything left to salvage.'

Jed nodded. 'Can you release a couple of drones on a city-wide sweep, include the city perimeter? I want to make sure we haven't missed anything.'

'Yep, doing it now.'

'And get me a link to the governor's office, will you?' Jed waited while Ash tapped quickly into his console and barely noticed the whine of the drones leaving the skimmer. *Where could an entire city of people go?* he thought. *Why wasn't there anyone here?*

'Here you go, Sir.'

'Thanks, Ash.' Jed looked at the small vid screen in front of him. The connection jumped twice before Martha's face appeared.

'Jed! You made good time. How is City 15? Have you met with the city officials yet?'

'Er no, not exactly.'

'Not exactly? What do you mean? What's happened?' Martha asked anxiously.

'There's no-one here. At least no-one obvious. We did a preliminary scan on approach, the city's forcefield was down. Upon entering we have been unable to establish any contact. There are no signs of life, Martha. Nothing.'

Martha looked blankly at Jed, trying to process the information. He waited for her to say something, but nothing was forthcoming.

'What do you want us to do?' he asked. Still no reply. 'Look, Martha, we're sending out some drones to do a city-wide scan, it might show something we missed. The air is clean so we'll send some teams out to investigate the medical centre, see if we can't find out what's happened.'

Martha fixed her gaze on him, finally coming to. 'Yes, yes, do that. Look for them, Jed. They can't have all disappeared. Not the entire city.'

'We will, Martha. I'll let you know as soon as we find anything. Over and out.' The connection jumped twice again as it disconnected making Jed suspicious. 'Was that a secure line, Ash?'

Ash looked up from his console. 'Secure into the governor's office but anyone with the right clearance could've listened in.'

'Can we try and get a more secure line next time? I don't know what we're going to find here, and the less people involved the better.'

'Yes, Sir,' said Ash.

Jed left him monitoring the drones and went to find the others.

Max was setting up a makeshift camp site for the non-operatives. It was nothing fancy, a few chairs and a small fold-up table. Somewhere for them to sit and wait a bit more comfortably than the inside of a skimmer. Kira had popped up Grace's play cube and the little girl was happily swiping at the walls, playing her interactive games without a care in the world. Dina handed Kira a cup of synth-caf which she took gratefully.

'What do you think has happened here?' Dina asked.

'I have no idea. It's all so...' Kira gestured round at the empty streets. 'So odd. I mean, where does an entire city go?'

They lapsed into silence, sipping their drinks and waiting. No-one sure what else to say.

It took about an hour for the full sweeps to come back. Ash called Jed over to the skimmer console.

'The entire city is empty, Sir. As expected, but see

this shape here on the perimeter sweep?'

Jed nodded.

'That's a biomass signature. It's faint but it's large. Hopefully that will give us an idea of what's happened or at least where everyone has gone.'

'How far away is it?' Jed asked.

'About twenty minutes, in that direction.' Ash pointed south. The opposite side to the city from where the expedition team had entered.

'Alpha Team - on me. We're heading out - full gear, two minutes!' Jed barked then lowered his voice to speak to Ash again. 'I want you to stay here, keep monitoring the scans, let me know if anything changes. Beta Team are on lookout patrol, so you've got fire power if anything happens. We'll radio in every half an hour.' He glanced over to Kira. 'Keep them safe, Ash.'

Ash nodded.

Jed picked up his gear and jogged over to the civilians. 'I'm heading out with Alpha Team, the perimeter sweep picked something up on the south side.' He addressed Max. 'Want to come, Doc?'

'Er, yeah, of course. Let me get my pack.' Max shoved his analyser into a nearby backpack and smiled crookedly at Kira, leaning in to kiss Dina on the head. 'Back soon!'

'What about me?' Dina was put out.

'I need you to stay here, with Kira and Grace. Keep monitoring the atmosphere. Let us know if anything changes but I'm sure we won't be long.' Jed gave Kira a quick hug and ruffled Grace's hair as she played in her cube before heading out with Max and the team of operatives.

'Do you think they'll be alright?' Dina asked watching them leave.

'Any synth-caf left?' asked Kira.

Dina looked at her in surprise then nodded and poured a fresh cup.

'Keep an eye on Grace, would you?' Kira took the cup and marched over to the skimmer where Ash still sat, eyes glued to his console. 'Hey, Ash, want some synth-caf?' Kira beamed at him.

'Er, yeah, sure. Thanks Ma'am.'

'Oh, call me Kira. We know each other well enough now. How are you doing?'

'Good thanks.' Ash smiled back at Kira, wondering why the sudden interest in his welfare.

'Family is important, isn't it, Ash?'

'Yes, yes of course it is. Is everything alright - is Grace okay?' Ash asked in alarm.

'Oh, she's fine, thanks. But it's important to know what our family is up to isn't it? So we can help to keep them safe.'

The penny dropped. 'You want to know where Alpha Team have gone. Here, look.' Ash showed Kira the dark shape on the perimeter of City 15's wall and Kira's stomach tightened in dread.

'Can we get a visual?'

'Um, yeah, I'm sure it will be alright.' Ash pushed a few buttons and Jed's cam feed sprang into life on the dashboard screen. Through a dark screen, it showed the skimmer passing buildings. They were still travelling to the southern side of the city. Ash and Kira watched the screen in silence.

'It's not exciting I'm afraid.'

'That's alright, Ash. This makes me feel like I'm there with him. Do you mind?' Kira gestured to the empty seat next to him and climbed into the skimmer. The passing buildings on screen began slowing down.

Alpha Team had arrived at their destination.

Jed's voice sounded tinny as he ordered the operatives out the skimmer and into standard formation, with him in the lead. They passed through the southern wall gateway and Kira cried out in surprise.

Chapter 8

'What the...' Jed looked at the scene in front of him in disbelief. Bodies lay on the ground. Not moving. His eyes darted frantically. There lay an elderly couple, nestled into each other on the brown, stubbly grass. Beyond them, a young couple with a small baby, recipients of recent collection. A group of Academy students were clustered together, handhelds still in their hands but screens wiped black. And over there, a familiar profile. It was Agent Devereaux. Dead with the rest of City 15. It didn't look real. It was as if every citizen had come outside the city walls and lain down to die. There was no blood, no wounds, no immediately obvious signs of distress. Just groups of people.

A crow landed on one of the bodies and walked up to the face where it proceeded to peck at the corpse. The bird raised its head triumphantly, a bloody eyeball hanging from its beak. There was a retching sound to Jed's left as one of the City Guard bent over to empty his stomach.

'Sorry, Sir.'

Jed waved away his apology. He didn't feel too clever either. 'Max, what happened here?'

Max's usual sunny disposition had vanished, he

looked pale under his permanent tan and was carefully scanning the area. 'Can you see this grass?'

Jed looked down at his feet in confusion. 'Yeah, there's grass. What of it?'

'What colour is it?'

'It's green, Max. For frag's sake! Don't we have bigger things to worry about than the colour of the grass?'

Max nodded to himself. 'Yes, it's green here but it's brown over there. As if it's been treated with something. Some kind of chemical maybe. But not airborne.' He checked his handheld. 'No, no toxins in the air.' He looked around swiftly. 'No immediate water supply either. So, were they doused from above?' He looked up. 'Possible, possible.'

'Max, what happened here?'

'Hmm?' Max didn't appear to realise he had been thinking out loud. 'I'm sorry, Jed. I don't know. I have a few theories, but I need to gather some samples and its delicate work. Could you go back for Dina for me? She's good in the field. I'll be fine here.'

Jed nodded and moved away reluctantly. He signalled for the Alpha Team Leader. 'Take the skimmer back and collect Dina please. Brief her on the situation and make sure she brings any and all equipment she needs. Take Hudson with you. I don't want his delicate stomach getting in the way. And don't, under any circumstances, bring my wife back with you.'

The operative saluted crisply and barked an order at Hudson. Without delay, the two men piled in the skimmer and sped away.

'The rest of you, I want a droid security perimeter set up outside the city wall. You lot watch inside the city. There may still be survivors,' said Jed.

'Sir, what happened here?'

'That is what we are going to find out. Now, get to work.'

The operatives fanned out, perimeter drones didn't take long to set up and Jed's team knew what they were doing. He was confident they would get on with it without the need for him to oversee them. He went back to Max.

'Max, I mean, have you ever...'

'Seen anything like this? Can't say I have, Jed. The only positives I can give you at the moment is that it looks like no-one suffered. But why they're dead I can't tell you.' Max shook his head. 'Without further tests, it's hard to say. It may be that time of death is fairly recent. I just don't know. I'm sorry.'

Jed nodded and the two men stood in quiet reflection for a moment, watching as more crows began circling the field.

'We need to get a body count. Is it safe?' Jed asked.

'It appears to be. I wouldn't touch anyone for now but walking past, getting a head count, should be fine. Shall I start this end?'

Jed nodded gratefully and strode off to the far side of the bodies. It was eerie. He kept expecting someone to move, kept thinking he saw something in the corner of his eye. But there was nothing. Each and everyone looked like they'd just lain down for a nap. It wasn't long before the two men met in the middle. They took a note of each other's numbers and then continued. When Max returned to the city walls with his final count, the skimmer had returned with Dina.

'I make it four hundred and twenty-eight - you?'

'Same.'

Dina hurried over, pale-faced but determined to do

65

whatever she needed. 'I bought the full sample kit. I wasn't sure what you'd want to test.' Her eyes strayed over to the bodies and she swallowed. 'Do we know anything?'

'Nothing I'd care to share without further investigation. Come on, we've got work to do.' Max gave her a brief hug and then opened up one of the cases she had brought. He extracted protective suits for them both to wear. Dina prepared the sample kits and once they'd both suited up, the two scientists bent to their task. They took samples of skin, hair, sediment from under the fingernails, swatches of cloth, made soil and grass solutions as well as taking samples of any food they could see. They tried to be random with their sampling yet followed a loose grid pattern to ensure they had something to test from across the site. It was getting dark by the time they'd finished.

'Do we need to worry about scavengers, Max?' Jed asked when they returned.

'It's a distinct possibility. I'm surprised we haven't seen anything more than the crows if I'm honest.'

'I'll set up a stasis field, then. Can you do the tests here, or do you need to go back to the other skimmer?'

'I think we should test here. I'd hate to bring back any potential contaminants.' Max looked back at the bodies. 'Whatever it is, it was done deliberately and clearly by someone these citizens trusted. There are no signs of violence whatsoever.'

Jed nodded grimly and left Max with Dina to sort out a quick field lab in order to process their samples. He went to the skimmer and activated the comms.

'Beta Camp. Beta Camp, Operative Ash, are you there?' asked Jed.

'Receiving you loud and clear, Sir.'

66

'As am I.' Kira's voice sounded strained.

Jed closed his eyes in dismay. He hadn't wanted her to see this.

'Jed, are you still there?' asked Kira.

'Yes, I'm still here.'

'What happened?'

'I don't know, love. We're running tests. Max and Dina will know more soon. Is Grace alright? Are you okay?'

'We're fine. Martha's sent a message. She wants an update.'

'What did you tell her?'

'Nothing, we haven't replied yet.'

'Please keep it that way. I'll report in and give her an update, don't worry. I'll let you know when we find anything out. I need to have a private word with Ash now, is that alright?'

'Yes hon, of course. I'll speak to you later?'

'Yep. Love you.'

'Love you too.'

There was a crackle and a fair amount of static as Kira unplugged herself from the comms system and climbed out of the skimmer, taking Grace with her. The baby began whimpering, she'd been happily playing with the skimmer belts in the back. Kira distracted her with an old-fashioned chew toy she had in her pocket. Grace's teeth were coming in and at least this way she could enjoy gnawing on a brightly coloured toy rather than endure semi-painful injections into her gums. Besides, they weren't even anywhere near a working med centre and there was no-one here to make those injections. Kira felt miserable, her heart aching for all those dead people she'd seen through Jed's cam.

'Ash, try and keep Kira busy. Away from here. I don't know how long this testing will take but I don't want too much traffic between the sites until I know there is no risk of contamination. If something happens out here, I need you to take Kira back to City 42. Understood?'

'Yes, Sir.'

'How much did she see?'

'Er, the bodies, Sir. We both saw the bodies before I cut the feed. Sorry, Sir.'

'It's alright. I need you to send a message to Governor Hamble to contact me on a secure line. In the interim, you're in charge of Beta Team. Make the camp secure, get the pods set up for sleeping and make sure you rotate a night watch.'

'Yes, Sir.'

'Oh, and I need a headcount for City 15 when you get a moment please.'

'I have that, Sir. It's four hundred and twenty-eight according to the Archive log. It's the only thing I've been able to hack so far.'

'Right. Thanks. I'll radio in again at 1900 hours but if you see anything, anything unusual, you get in touch. Understood.'

'Yes, Sir.'

'Over and out.'

Kira and Grace were waiting outside the skimmer when Ash opened the door.

'What did he say?'

'Um, they are staying there to run the analysis. In case of contamination.' Ash replied.

'Okay, so we're meant to stay here and camp in the plaza?'

'That's about the size of it, Ma'am.'

'Don't Ma'am me, Ash. Kira is fine. Can we get a comms link back to City 42? To Martha's office?'

Feeling relieved that Kira wasn't asking about the other campsite, Ash nodded and turned back to establish a connection. He pulled the screen out and round so Kira could see from outside the skimmer. It took longer than expected but eventually he'd managed to open a channel to Martha's office.

'Here you go, it's ready when you are. Can you ask the governor to check her secure messages as well, please? There should be one from us, telling her to contact Captain Jenkins in the field.'

'Yes, of course. Thanks, Ash.'

'Also...'

'You don't want me to mention the bodies, do you?' asked Kira, her voice quiet.

'No Ma'am. We should wait for the Captain to report in.' Ash was relieved she'd mentioned it first. He didn't want to tell Mrs Jenkins what she could and couldn't say.

'It's okay, Ash. I won't tell her what we've seen. I just want to talk to her.' Kira peered through the static as the connection stabilised, she was barely able to make out a desk and a shadowy shape. 'Martha? Are you there?'

'Who is this?' It was a man's voice. Kira couldn't quite place him, but he sounded familiar.

'Kira Jenkins. Who is this? Where's Martha?'

'Ms Hamble is... unavailable for comment.' And the line went dead. Kira blinked in surprise. What was all that about? She turned to look for Ash to tell him what happened, but he was helping the rest of Beta Team make up the sleeping pods for the night. Perhaps Kira had tried at a bad time. She carried Grace over to one of the larger pods and was relieved to see her cube already set up. A good night's sleep. That's what everyone needed. Kira began sorting out her daughter for bed, hoping things would seem clearer in the morning.

ENCRYPTED MESSAGE FROM NEW CORP TO 7421
>>IMPLEMENT OPERATION VNC - CONFIRM<<

ENCRYPTED MESSAGE FROM 7421 TO NEW CORP
>>Absolutely confirmed! You won't be disappointed<<

Chapter 9

*C42N: No news from City 15. Do you have an update?
Sweep what you know.*

*SMAC: The Governor will release a statement about
City 15.*

*ANON17: What's going on? They should've been there
by now! Who's keeping secrets? Together they're telling
us lies!*

'Who was that on the comms?' Martha frowned at Sean
as she came back into her office. She was sure she'd seen
Kira's face on the screen behind him, but the image had
been distorted so it was difficult to know for sure.

'No-one, Ma'am. A poor connection with the news
feed. Seems we're having static issues.'

'Wonderful,' said Martha. 'I suppose we'd better add
that to the long list of things to resolve.'

'Yes, Ma'am.'

'That was meant to be rhetorical, Sean.'

'Yes, Ma'am.'

Martha pinched her nose and closed her eyes briefly.
She had never warmed to Sean. He was efficient at his

job, invaluable really, but he always seemed to be lurking at the edges of City 42's latest disaster. Ruth was convinced he was going to make a play for power but so far all he'd done was simply be everywhere. Usually before Martha had the chance to respond publicly and often with all the information at his fingertips, before she had even had chance to review the latest reports. With herself and Ruth feeling exhausted all the time Martha supposed it was important to have at least one fully capable team member. Stimulants only went so far and when their effects wore off, she often felt worse than she had before.

'Sean, have we heard from the expedition team at City 15 yet?'

'No, Ma'am.'

'So why did you sweep about the update? Without my authority?'

'There was a lot of negative chatter on the Sweeps, Ma'am. I thought we'd get ahead of it, for once,' Sean replied.

Martha couldn't fault his logic.

'Next time, run it past me first, please. All sweeps from government officials have to be pre-approved, you know that - it was your idea,' she said.

'Yes, Ma'am.' Sean cocked his head to one side as he checked his handheld. 'There is only one more meeting today - about the waste removal system. Why don't you let me deal with that and I'll let you know if the team check in. You look tired.'

Martha bristled slightly. She knew she looked tired, she didn't need to be reminded about it but her sensible side was leaping with joy at the thought of being able to leave the office early or at least on time for once.

'Are you sure you're happy to take that meeting solo?

It's fairly routine, so there shouldn't be anything untoward and you can ping me instantly if anything...'

Sean broke in smoothly. 'It will be fine. Go. Relax. I've got everything covered.'

Martha felt like she was being dismissed but chalked it up to being tired and overreacting. She gathered her handheld and her jacket and smiled gratefully at Sean as they both walked to her office door. After all, he was only trying to help. She stopped at the door and turned to him.

'One more thing, Sean. How many babies are left in the growth labs?' asked Martha, hoping that she hadn't already asked him that question today. The earlier meeting had reminded her that there were still a few collections left. She was so tired, she thought if she closed her eyes, she might never wake up again.

'Seven, plus one unclaimed in the lab,' Sean replied.

'Unclaimed? How did that happen? Don't we have a waiting list?' Martha rubbed her temple with one hand, swiping her handheld with the other, trying to find the report.

'I can't speak for my predecessor.' Sean was calm, cool and collected, as always. 'But yes, there is an unclaimed child in the lab.' He checked his own handheld. 'Looks like mixed race, four months old.' He looked up at Martha. 'I can have it reassigned.'

'It? Boy or girl, Sean?'

'Er, boy.'

Martha felt a pang of sadness. The same age as Pete and Ingrid's baby, if it had survived. And mixed race. She started to feel more awake as she considered the possibility. No. It couldn't be. Could it?

'Can you transfer that file over to my personal handheld please?'

'The orphan? Why?'

'Thank you, Sean. As for the babies left in the growth lab, have they all been assigned?'

The lines around Sean's mouth tightened momentarily before he replied. 'Yes, but we have eight families petitioning for new ones to be grown. They're getting more and more support daily for reopening the labs. Couldn't the orphan could be sent off to one of them?'

'I want to look into where he came from first. Thank you, Sean. Is there anything else?' Martha hoped not.

'No, Ma'am. But we do need to discuss the baby lab reopening...'

'Tomorrow, Sean. Tomorrow.'

He nodded, swiped his handheld and flashed a half grin at Martha as he left her to lock her office behind them.

Checking the time Martha realised that it was already past the end of normal office hours. She pinged her friend.

'Are Lucas and Sarah alright?'

'Yeah, they're fine. You finished already?'

'On way now, just need to check one thing.'

'Don't be too late.'

Martha smiled, feeling lighter. For once she had an earlier finish than usual and time to spend with her son. It was looking like a good evening ahead. As soon as she'd looked into the orphaned boy situation.

MSCHILD: *Governor Hamble consistently refuses to discuss reopening the growth labs. Who does she think she is? Just because she had her baby.*
It's not fair.

Sean smiled at the collection of people around the table. They were what was left of the Corporation supporters in City 42. Those who had held powerful positions before the uprising and had now been left to obscurity. It was true, some had made it onto Governor Hamble's advisory team but in low level positions. He would still have to be wary of them, if they didn't feel like they were being offered something more than they already had they might inform Martha of what was happening here today. And Sean wasn't quite ready for that, yet.

'Gentlemen, Ladies, let's open the discussion, shall we? First item of business - level of confidence in the current administration.'

Chapter 10

*C42N: Do you think we should have an election?
Join the conversation in social hub beta.*

*ANON17: GOVHAM can't even attend her own
meetings. What can possibly be more important?*

*SMAC: Waste management is at the top of the
Governor's agenda.*

Martha pinged Ruth again but there was no reply. That
was nothing new. She probably had her hands full with
Sarah and Lucas. Martha felt a pang of guilt for not
being at home with her baby, but their childcare
arrangement was part of their working agreement. Ruth
shouldered the bulk of childcare whilst Martha focused
on her role as governor of City 42. So far, so good, but it
was only a temporary fix. They would have to come up
with something more permanent, especially if Martha's
hunch was right.

She thanked Gaia that the baby lab was in the same
building as her office, she didn't think she could bear to
travel half-way across the city to find out whether she
was right or not.

Inside the baby lab, the seven infants that were still growing pulsed gently within their synthetic cocoons. Such a peaceful environment thought Martha as she looked for a staff member. There should always be someone on duty but there didn't seem to be anyone here. A low rumbling noise was coming from the left-hand side of the room. Martha went over to investigate.

There, in the large cube, designed for sleeping multiple infants, a grown man lay snoring. A baby was tucked into the crook of his arm and was also peacefully sleeping. It was a surprising scene yet one that tugged Martha's heartstrings. She too wished she could nap so contentedly, with her baby but, she never seemed to have the time. She cleared her throat and the snoozing giant snorted then opened his eyes.

'Don't wake the baby,' he whispered as he extended the crook of his arm, releasing the child from his embrace and snuggling him into a pile of nearby blankets. Then there was a rather inelegant scramble for the man to get up off the floor and out of the cube. He stretched his neck making it crack loudly then peered intently at his visitor. 'Do I know you?'

'I hope so. Governor Hamble.' Martha extended her hand and smiled warmly at the surprised look on the man's face.

He hurriedly wiped his hands on his trousers and then double shook Martha's hand. 'Marty, Miss Hamble. An honour to meet you. Great to see you here. An honour, truly an honour. How can I help you? You don't need another baby, do you? I mean, you already have one, don't you.' He trailed off, realising that what he was saying wasn't coming out quite right. He tried again. 'Governor Hamble, what can I do for you?'

She smiled at him, letting him know that he wasn't in

any kind of trouble, then pointed to the child in the cube.

'What can you tell me about this baby?'

Marty looked at the little boy. 'Well, bit of an odd one this. He came to us from Corp Medical, about four months ago. It was around the time of the terrorist attack, so we figured the family who were assigned him had perished in the tragedy.'

'Why wasn't he reported?'

'Ah, well, you see. There was a lot of confusion after the terrorist attack. We lost valuable staff members and then the computer lock-down didn't help. It was tricky to back track the files, find out who this little fella belongs to and then of course your governorship came into being and it all sort of, well...' He trailed off not entirely sure how to explain what had happened.

'This little guy got lost in the system.' Martha's eyes filled with tears. 'Has he been well looked after?'

'Yes, yes, of course. We all cherish him dearly. Mr Sean knows all about him of course. He told us the little lad would be reassigned soon.'

'I see.' Martha's brain whirled. Surely Sean should've bought this information to her sooner. It felt like he had been trying to hide it. But to what end? 'I'd like to take him home with me. What do I need to do?'

'Er, Governor Hamble, um, that's kind of you but, don't you already have a child at home?'

'I do.' Martha waited to see what the man would say next. She wasn't sure she should be doing this, but she needed to take the baby home. She had to know if her hunch was right.

C42N: GOVHAM leaves Hamble HQ with new baby.

MSCHILD: How dare Hamble take that baby! She

79

already has one. Who else is she screwing over? It should've been mine!

ANON17: Hamble is a baby-stealer. I bet she's still selling them.

'Where have you been?' Ruth sounded harassed. The children had been irritable, when one stopped mithering, the other one started. It was as though they had an evil plan. She stopped in her tracks, mouth open in surprise when she saw Martha carrying another baby. 'Is there something you want to tell me?'

'I think this is Ingrid and Pete's child.'

Ruth went pale and dropped to sit in a nearby chair. 'How?'

'I don't know.'

'What the frag happened after I left today?'

'I was wrapping things up with Sean and I was discussing how many babies were left in the baby lab and who was still on the waiting list, when he mentioned an uncollected baby.'

'Uncollected? But that would never happen. I know of at least five families desperate for a child who aren't even on the waiting list.'

Martha clutched the sleeping baby closer to her. 'Is it still that bad?'

'Women aren't falling pregnant, Ma. It was just us, and nobody else since. There's a lot of unhappy people out there. And finding out about the hundreds of babies that were grown and shipped out has horrified everyone.'

'That's not my fault. No-one knew about it, just like the treated water.'

'Yeah, but the discovery was made under your government,' said Ruth. 'People are stupid, Ma. They

80

blame you even though they know you didn't really have anything to do with it.'

'I know, you're right. We are trying to get to the bottom of it. The scientists are doing everything they can to figure out the long-term effects of the irradiated water and as soon as we crack the computers, we'll find out why the city was selling babies.'

'If we crack the computers,' said Ruth.

The women lapsed into silence as they considered one of the biggest threats to Martha's governorship. If she couldn't explain why Corporation had been selling babies without telling anyone and solve the problem of women not falling pregnant soon, then she was going to lose a huge support base.

'A lot of people still think you're doing that,' said Ruth.

'Doing what?' asked Martha.

'Selling babies.'

'And who exactly am I selling all these babies to?'

Ruth shrugged and turned her attention to the baby in Martha's arms. 'What makes you think it's Pete's?' she asked.

'Well, he's mixed race, not unusual I know but that is what their baby would've been. He's the right age, again - it could be a coincidence but when I spoke to the tech in the baby lab it seemed to click into place. The child was bought there shortly after the terrorist attack. The one that Ingrid...'

'But we all saw the footage, thanks to Anti-Corp. On the sweeps. The doctors confirming the termination of mother and child.'

'Yes, but we never actually saw them terminate the child, did we? And they never released the bodies for the funeral. We looked throughout Corp Medical for some

81

kind of sign that those bodies had been kept and found nothing.'

Ruth rolled her eyes. 'Are you suggesting that Ingrid is still alive, as well? Died her hair brown, working in some menial job somewhere, biding her time before taking back her baby?'

'No, of course no. Don't be so melodramatic.'

'Look, I know you feel bad about the baby situation, but you can't latch on to an uncollected child and decide it's Pete and Ingrid's baby. You just can't. You need proof, Ma.'

'I am well aware of that. We are going to run a DNA test.'

'What? Here?' Ruth was incredulous.

'Yes.'

'How?'

Martha smiled grimly and went through to her bedroom. When she returned, a NanNan 3000 was following her.

'Where did you get that from?' Ruth was surprised.

'Kira gave it to me. It was the last present Ingrid ever brought her and Jed. I don't think either of them could bear to get rid of it, but they had no use for it either.'

'And it does DNA testing?'

'Let's find out, shall we?' Martha was still holding the baby in her arms and seemed reluctant to put him down. As if he would disappear if she did. One handed, she opened the medical diagnostics app on the NanNan, scrolling until she found what she was looking for. DNA test.

'Hang on a minute though, Ma. We don't have any of Ingrid or Pete's DNA and there is no central network anymore. How will the NanNan be able to tell us anything useful?' asked Ruth.

'Jed has their personnel files. Backed up into his personal system, which I have emergency access to. Kira told me about it when she caught him looking at their individual data streams.' Martha's voice went soft. 'Apparently it helped him feel connected to them still.'

'So, we're really doing this then? We're going to test this kid to see if it's Ingrid and Pete's?'

Martha nodded resolutely. The NanNan was ready, she hit the button for the scan and watched nervously as the android took a hair sample from the small baby. It took mere moments to process the hair and the results were soon available to download. Saving the data to her handheld, Martha went over to the main screen in the living room and accessed the Jenkins' personal system.

Ruth looked round nervously, knowing that Kira and Jed were miles away in City 15, but still feeling like she was prying into their personal privacy uninvited. 'I don't know about this, Ma.'

'Oh hush.' Martha navigated the system expertly, finding the DNA profiles quickly and then holding up the recent scan from the child.

The two women looked at the patterns in front of them. Despite Ruth being a history teacher and Martha originally a plant biologist by trade, it was clear that the child's DNA had matching bands with his parents. Ingrid Jenkins and Pete Barnes.

Martha looked down at the baby in her arms. 'He is. He's Pete and Ingrid's baby.'

Ruth looked like she'd seen a ghost. 'We have to tell Jed, and Kira. Can we get in contact with them?'

Martha nodded.

'I think so. They took the latest comm units with them so provided they're not in a location with high interference, we should be alright.'

'Do we tell them now?' asked Ruth.

'Yes. What are we waiting for?'

'I don't know but should we wait for them to come back? I mean, isn't this mission, expedition, whatever you want to call it, highly critical? Don't we want them focused on the field and not wanting to rush back home?' Ruth sounded dubious.

Martha was quiet. She wanted to scream it from the rooftops, but Ruth might have a point. It wouldn't do much good to distract Jed while he was on mission. They should wait before telling him. The baby began to fidget in her arms.

'Do we have enough supplies for another one?' Martha asked Ruth, just as Sarah, then Lucas began to cry.

'I guess we'll find out,' sighed Ruth. Being a mum to three babies loomed ahead of her and she didn't think she particularly relished the prospect.

ENCRYPTED MESSAGE FROM 7421 TO NEW CORP

>>*URGENT - Hamble has discovered the child, what do I do?*<<

ENCRYPTED MESSAGE FROM NEW CORP TO 7421

>>EVIDENTLY, YOUR INCOMPETENCE KNOWS NO BOUNDS. THE CHILD SHOULD'VE BEEN DEALT WITH MONTHS AGO<<
>>DO NOTHING. I WILL DEAL WITH IT<<

ENCRYPTED MESSAGE FROM 7421 TO NEW CORP

>>*What about City 15? They've found the bodies. I can't keep it from the Governor for much longer*<<

ENCRYPTED MESSAGE FROM NEW CORP TO 7421

>>DO WE HAVE SUPPORT?<<

ENCRYPTED MESSAGE FROM 7421 TO NEW CORP

>>*Yes, most of the old Corpers are open to the idea of a new leadership. What do you want me to do next?*<<

ENCRYPTED MESSAGE FROM NEW CORP TO 7421

>>HOLD THE VOTE<<

Chapter 11

'I want to do something useful,' announced Kira.

Ash looked up in surprise. He had thought she'd turned in for the night. 'What sort of thing are you thinking?' he asked cautiously.

'I think we should go look for medical supplies. After all, that is one of the reasons we came here in the first place.'

'True, but now is not the best time.'

'No, I don't mean now, this minute. Of course not. It's night-time. But I think first thing in the morning you, me, and a couple of operatives should go to 15's med centre and see what's left.'

'I'll have to get it confirmed with Captain Jenkins, but I can't see any real issue with it.' Ash thought for a moment. 'But doesn't Dina have the list of medicines we need?'

'I have a copy as well. I know what we need to get.' Kira was beaming. She hated feeling like she had nothing to do. This would give her purpose. It would also get them moving around the city which would divert Grace's attention from trying to eat skimmer tread and playing with spare Force riot gear stored in the transporters.

'I'll radio through, let you know.' Ash waited until Kira had gone before setting up the comms link with Alpha Team.

'Alpha Team, Alpha Team. This is Operative Ash, Beta Camp - do you read me? Over.'

'Loud and clear, Ash. This is Captain Jenkins. Switching to visual comms. Over.'

The vid screen in the transporter flickered and Jed's head came slowly into view. The connection wasn't the best but at least they had visual comms.

'How are things there, Ash?'

'Everything's fine, Sir. Perimeter is set, night watch has been organised. The team have eaten, those not on duty are resting. Your wife is fine, she's turned in for the night with your daughter. We don't anticipate any problems.'

'Good, good. Max and Dina are still running analysis here. It will probably take another twelve to fourteen hours. I need you to sit tight for now.'

'Actually, Sir, I was wondering whether Beta Team could visit the Med Centre, see if there are any supplies available. That was our secondary mission after all.'

'It was.' Jed thought for a moment. 'OK, do it. Take Kira and Grace with you, give them a protective detail at all times. I'm not expecting any trouble but that's usually when it hits. Do you have the list of meds we need?'

'Yes, Sir. At least, your wife does, Sir.'

'Ah. Okay.' Jed grinned. 'Try not to let her get you into too much trouble, Ash.'

'Yes, Sir.' Ash grinned back at his commanding officer. They said goodnight and signed off the comms. Nothing to do now but try and sleep peacefully until morning.

No-one slept much in the end and Beta Team broke

camp early, packing everything away into one skimmer and emptying out the other one as much as possible. Everyone was feeling optimistic that they would be filling the empty skimmer's containers and storage areas with medical supplies.

'We are going to walk there, aren't we?' Kira asked Ash anxiously. She didn't feel like being cooped up in that vehicle for a minute longer than necessary.

'We can do, Ma'am. We won't all fit in anyway.' Ash smiled then looked down at Grace who was trying her best to pull herself up to standing on a nearby box of dried food pouches. 'What about Grace?'

'Oh, don't worry. I have her stroller. If we waited for her to toddle to the Med Centre, we'd be waiting all day.' In a few deft moves, Kira undid the contraption lying on the floor next to her and with an expert flick of her wrist, a fully functional stroller now stood waiting for its passenger.

'Impressive. They fold up well, don't they?' Ash said.

'Believe me, the first time you try to undo these things, it takes you half an hour but with a little one, you get plenty of practice getting the stroller in and out of skimmers.' Kira scooped up Grace and secured her into the seat. 'Are we ready?'

Ash nodded then called the order to move out. Half of Beta Team were to stay there and guard the camp whilst the rest were to come to the med centre, the empty skimmer following the human crocodile. Kira noticed with a faint smile that the most heavily armed operatives surrounded her and Grace. She didn't mind. This was Jed's way of making sure she was safe. The impending doom feeling she had had yesterday was gone. Kira knew Max and Dina would get to the bottom of what happened to the citizens of 15. Now she felt an odd sort of an excitement. She was on an exploratory mission to find much needed medical supplies and she could think of no reason why the supplies they were looking for wouldn't be there. It felt good to be part of such a positive action.

Two hours later, Kira and Ash sat dejectedly on the benches outside the med centre. It wasn't a particularly big building and it hadn't taken Beta Team long to scout through. It was completely empty. There were beds, tables and chairs but all the electronics had been ripped out and taken away. Every single medical cabinet was cleaned out. Not even a handheld med scanner had been left behind. Kira's mind was spinning. Who had the kind of manpower to empty out a med centre so efficiently? Was it Corporation? Had they somehow expected City 42 to send an envoy and instead of agreeing to meet, they had instead decided to remove anything and everything that could've been helpful? They had even taken small things like child plasters and the holographic stickers they loved so much. All the food hydrators had been shut down and without the city key codes, Ash had been unable to get anything turned back on. Thank goodness someone had considered that eventuality and brought enough supplies with them for the entire expedition.

Ash tapped at his handheld despondently. All his scans had come back negative. There were no harmful elements in the air or anything contaminating the building. It was completely empty.

'I suppose we ought to report into Jed.' Kira spoke at last.

Ash nodded and walked back to the still empty skimmer. So much for thinking they would be able to achieve something positive today.

89

'Alpha Team. Alpha Team come in please. This is Beta Team. Operative Ash speaking. Over.'

'Beta Team received, this is Captain Jenkins. Switching to visual. Over.'

The vid comm on the dash flickered once more into life and Jed's hopeful face looked out. He was soon frowning.

'The entire place is empty? Actually empty?'

'Yes, Sir. There is some furniture but otherwise nothing is left. No food, no water, no medical supplies and no access to the city's mainframe.'

'Any sign as to who did this?'

'No, Sir. There are no messages left behind or even any real evidence that anyone was here in the first place. Just an empty building.'

'And you're sure there aren't any contaminants?'

'No, Sir. No contaminants.'

There was a pause as Jed digested the information. They had completely failed in their medical re-supply mission and the mysterious deaths of the entire population of City 15 was the absolute worst possible scenario. Trying to explain what they'd found to City 42 wouldn't help Martha's position at all.

'Go back to camp, Ash. Get the skimmers ready to move out. We are on our way back as well. If you can think of anywhere else to investigate before we leave, let me know but I think we've done everything here we can.'

'Yes, Sir. See you back at camp, Sir.'

Chapter 12

'Are the results in?' Jed asked as he poked his head under the tarpaulin Max and Dina had rigged up to keep their testing under some kind of shelter. Not that the weather was bad here in City 15 but more to limit the chances of any kind of contamination. Dina's eyes were rimmed in red as she looked up at Jed and nodded. She didn't speak. She wasn't sure she could. Max squeezed her shoulder as he stood upright, his lanky form towering over both of them.

'They were poisoned. Looks like it came through the city's airways, most likely at some point in the evening which is why we see the grouping we do. Families together, students, work colleagues, that sort of thing,' he explained.

'What about the individual bodies?' asked Jed.

'I'm guessing they were gassed in the street. Anyone who was inside a building would've been affected at the same time,' replied Max.

'Do you think it was a complete city-wide assault? All at once?'

'It looks that way. From what we've been able to determine, time of death is pretty much the same across the board.'

'And they didn't miss a single person,' said Dina quietly. 'Our count matches the city's population. Every single resident was targeted.'

Jed was quiet for a moment then asked the obvious question. 'So why aren't they in their homes or wherever they happened to be when the airborne assault occurred?'

'I think, and this is pure conjecture, that the bodies were removed from the city and placed outside the city walls to be destroyed,' said Max. 'I believe the discolouration in the grass is down to an accelerant, I think we arrived before they were able to complete that task. Whoever they are.'

Jed shook his head in disbelief. He began pacing up and down. 'We interrupted them? Why haven't they finished us off as well? Where are they?'

Dina tapped one of the monitors, bringing up their analysis for Jed. 'It looks like the toxin they used was fast acting and quick to break down. In some of the later samples we collected and tested there were only trace amounts of the poison left. If we hadn't known what to look for, we would have missed it.'

'Are you telling me that they, what, ran out of poison?' Jed sounded annoyed. 'Whoever did this clearly doesn't have an issue with killing people. If we interrupted them, why weren't we attacked? There's not that many of us, they could have wiped all of us out with a few well-placed snipers.'

Max shook his head and gestured to the outer wall. 'I think the poison was released by drone, remotely.'

'Remotely? By whom?' asked Jed.

'I don't know.'

'Okay, so let's say for a moment that's exactly what happened, what about the bodies? How did they get here?' Jed jabbed a finger towards the southern wall that hid the mass genocide of City 15.

'I'm not sure,' Max replied. 'It may be that they were teleported somehow...' But Jed interrupted him.

'Teleported? What, some kind of alien ship came along and moved all our people for no fragging reason?'

Dina caught hold of one of Jed's arms that was gesturing wildly. 'Jed, hey, calm down. Listen to Max's theory. We're trying to help.'

Max had stepped back, a little out of the way, and he hovered protectively behind Dina. 'Look, Jed. I don't have the answers. I don't know what happened here but someone extremely powerful and resourceful gassed an entire city. For whatever reason the tech they used to do this is nowhere to be seen. But I think it's safe to say that they will be back. We should leave. Now.'

Jed stared at Max for a long moment, unable to fully comprehend what he was saying. 'Who would do this... not Corporation, surely?' he murmured.

'We don't know what Corporation is capable of,' Dina retorted. 'But Max is right, we need to pack up and leave. Whoever did this will easily be able to deal with us.'

Jed started nodding and began yelling instructions as he walked away from the makeshift lab. Alpha Team scurried to collect and stow all their gear whilst Max and Dina swiftly packed away all their samples and equipment.

'What about the dead bodies, Max?' Dina asked quietly as they worked quickly.

'Nature will do what nature does.'

Dina rubbed her eyes, trying not to cry. 'It feels so wrong to leave them out there like that.'

'I know but we can't risk the time it would take to dig a grave for them all.'

'We could burn them.' Dina turned her tear-stained face up to him, eyes filled with hope that he would agree.

Max nodded. 'Yes, we could burn them.' He hugged Dina briefly then jogged over to Jed and started gesturing expansively. Dina watched Jed's face as he listened to Max. There was a brief flash of pain and a tight nod. Max came back to Dina.

'He says pack it all up then he'll get his team to, well, do what's necessary.'

Dina nodded and wiped her nose on her sleeve. 'We'll bear witness and send their souls on. Gaia would want that.'

The camp quickly became nothing more than a skimmer and a few scuffs in the ground to show that someone had been there. Max had identified the accelerant as a simple bio liquid, one they themselves used for various things. There was more of it in the skimmer, so Jed ordered Alpha Team to spray the field of dead again. The team stood for a moment, heads bowed, keeping their thoughts to themselves.

Dina whispered a small prayer. 'Honour the earth, honour the sky, honour the water, honour Gaia who watches over us, honour all those we share this planet with. Send these souls to her loving embrace, we will remember you.' Her eyes filled with tears that sprang down her cheeks and fell to the ground, but she didn't care. She was horrified to have witnessed such an atrocity, scared that they might all be in danger and deeply saddened that so many people had lost their lives at the whim of an unknown enemy.

There was a soft whoosh as Jed lit the first fire. Other operatives lit strategic points around the grave site and they all watched for a moment as the flames took hold, licking greedily at the bodies.

'C'mon, we don't need to stay to the end.' Max steered Dina away from the mass cremation and gently manoeuvred her into the skimmer. Soon they were all travelling away from the southern wall of City 15, back towards Kira and Grace and the rest of the team at Central Plaza.

Jed had tried to report in to Martha using the small comms system he had but there must have been some kind of interference as nothing was going through. He would have to report on the bigger comms array in the other skimmer. But he could do that as they left the city. After Max's revelation he had no desire to hang around and be the next series of victims to the nameless enemy that had destroyed City 15.

Jed was relieved when he saw Kira waving at him as they returned to the first camp site. It looked like Ash had received the brief message telling him to get everything packed up ready to go as there nothing in the plaza apart from the skimmer. He quickly ran over and swept his wife up into a huge hug. She looked a little surprised yet pleased.

'So, what happened?' asked Kira.

'We'll fill you in on the way but we're getting out of here first.' Jed looked back over his shoulder and called for Dina and Max to get in the second skimmer with him, Ash, Kira and of course, Grace. They would take the science supplies and kit bags etc. It meant all the operatives were travelling together but Jed wanted to have a frank conversation with Martha and the fewer ears listening in, the better.

'Roll out,' Jed ordered.

The two skimmers began travelling out of the city. A single spy drone watched them, unnoticed, from the sky above. Its recorder blinking, transmitting data back to its source.

Jed tried to connect his call through to Martha's office, but it wasn't until the skimmer had left the outer walls of City 15 that the connection held. Martha's face swam into view, her eyes looked bruised with dark shadows beneath them and her forehead was wrinkled in a concerned frown.

'Jed! Finally! We've been trying to get hold of you for hours. I need a report for the board. What is the situation in City 15?'

'Martha.' Jed nodded a greeting. He angled the comm screen so he could talk to her directly without either of them being distracted by the passengers in the back of the skimmer. He needn't have worried as Kira was grilling Max and Dina about everything they'd seen at the wall and wasn't paying attention to Jed.

'Obviously I'll file a full report but, I've never seen anything like it, Ma.'

Martha knew it must be serious, Jed rarely shortened her name except in times of crisis. She schooled her face to stillness and listened attentively as Jed began his report, relaying what they had initially found, namely the lack of any life signs.

'No life signs at all?' Martha interrupted then apologised and gestured for Jed to continue.

'Operative Ash discovered an unusual biomass signature outside the southern wall of the city so Alpha Team, including myself, Max and Dina went to investigate. Beta Team, headed up by Operative Ash and Kira, remained behind. They went to investigate the Med Centre but found nothing, it had been completely emptied of all supplies.'

Martha's face paled.

'Alpha Team travelled to the southern exit of the city and discovered the entire population of City 15 outside the city walls.'

Martha breathed a sigh of relief. 'What were they doing out there? They weren't hiding from us, were they?'

Jed shook his head. 'No, Ma. They were all dead.'

There was a long silence.

'Dead?' asked Martha in disbelief.

'Yes. Max and Dina performed a series of experiments to determine the cause of death and discovered it was an airborne poison.'

'But not everyone? Not every single person was dead, surely?' Martha interrupted again.

Jed gave a curt nod and continued with his report. 'Max's theory is that the bodies were removed immediately post-mortem by some kind of transporter technology although we have no proof of that.'

'Did they... were they... had they suffered?' Martha's eyes glinted wetly.

'They looked peaceful. Arranged in their family or friend groupings.'

'What did you do with them?'

'We burnt them.'

Martha blinked rapidly in surprise. And then slowly nodded. She knew he was right; they couldn't leave all those people lying out there. It was disrespectful to their memory. She could barely believe it though, such a huge loss of life. How was she going to tell the citizens of City 42 what happened? Could she keep them safe against a similar attack?

'How long until you get back?' she finally managed to ask.

'I'm not sure to be honest, we left in a hurry. We

might regroup at Camp Eden before heading back into the city - with your permission, of course. Max and Dina want the chance to put together their notes for the official report.'

Martha nodded distractedly, 'Yes, yes, of course.' She knew she had to tell Jed about Pete and Ingrid's baby but now didn't seem to be the moment. One of her aides appeared in the doorway of her office, gesturing frantically, desperately trying to get Martha's attention. She held up one finger to the young woman.

'Jed, I have to go. Is there anything else pertinent I should know before going into this meeting?'

'No, Martha. You have the facts. I am sorry to have been the bearer of such grim news.'

'And you've got no idea who was behind this?'

Jed shook his head. 'I can only guess at Corporation, but I never thought they would be this ruthless. Especially to a city that wasn't in direct uprising. It makes me nervous, Martha. I'm not sure that being in City 42 is particularly safe for anyone now. If they, whoever they are, can do that to City 15 without raising any alarms, it doesn't seem like a big leap to wipe us out as well.'

Martha privately agreed with him but said nothing further, instead she said her goodbyes and signed off. Her aide looked like she was about to faint with relief at finally being able to interrupt her boss.

Chapter 13

C42N: An emergency board meeting has been called - what happened in City 15? Join the conversation in social hub beta.

ANON17: What's gone wrong now?

SMAC: Board meetings are normal. We will release the usual update after the meeting.

CORPTECH2: Give us back our jobs!

MSCHILD: Stop stealing babies! Give us proper leadership!

ANON40: Hamble to resign! Hamble to resign!

'Ma'am? They've called an emergency meeting, Ma'am. Everyone's already there. And... and...'

'Yes, I know,' said Martha. 'The board is meeting as usual this afternoon. I'd hardly call it an emergency, Jess.'

'No, Ma'am, that's not it at all - they're all in there now, talking about you. And Sean is running the meeting. I really think you need to be there.' The young aide's brow was creased with worry.

At hearing that, Martha quickly stood up, gripping her handheld tightly, her thoughts spiralling wildly. She had thought the board were convening a meeting to discuss the results of the expedition out to City 15. But she hadn't submitted her report yet and that meeting was meant to be later this afternoon, not now. This sounded like something else. Martha started to feel cross. Who did Sean think he was, calling an emergency meeting like this without any consultation whatsoever?

Martha entered the board room with as much dignity as she could muster after practically running down the corridor. She slowed her pace in surprise at what she saw. Every seat was full, and Sean was running the meeting from her chair. He looked comfortable and at ease. Her stomach prickled nervously. She tried to make sense of what was happening. Ruth wasn't there, neither was Chief Minkov from Force and Dr Lee refused to look her in the eye.

'Ladies, Gentlemen.' Martha greeted the room then turned to her chair. 'Sean? Is there something I should know?'

'Martha, so good of you to join us.' Sean looked slowly around the room and then faced her with a little smirk and a small shrug of his shoulders. 'There doesn't appear to be a chair for you.'

Martha ignored his comment. 'Why has this meeting been called?'

'Well... we're voting.'

'And what exactly are you voting on?'

'Your fitness to be governor,' replied Sean with a look of satisfaction.

Martha blanched and steadied herself on the back of

a chair. That was unexpected. Sean smiled.

'We were totting up the results. Now, where were we?'

An administrative assistant whom Martha recognised but couldn't for the life of her remember who he was, cleared his throat and gave a little nod in Sean's direction. 'On the matter of confidence in the current governor, we have twenty nays, three yays, one non-attendance and no abstainers.'

'I'm sorry Ms Hamble, it appears your government do not think you are fit to run this city. Someone will help you clear out your desk.' Sean gestured to one of the men standing around the outskirts of the room. Martha realised it was a security guard, but he wasn't dressed in Force uniform. His jumpsuit was emblazoned with a large C. Was he a Corporation security guard? Here, in her board room? What the hell was going on? She held up her hand to stop the guard's progress towards her.

'That won't be necessary thank you, Sean. I am perfectly capable of collecting my personal effects by myself.'

'It's not that we don't trust you, but you see, we don't trust you.' Sean jabbed a finger aggressively in her direction while addressing the room. 'Because, not only did Ms Hamble have full knowledge of the additional babies her father sanctioned for creation and sale - elsewhere, not here in City 42 where many families are desperate for children of their own,' he paused for breath. 'She removed a child from the baby lab yesterday, without going through the proper channels.' He turned to face her. 'When exactly are you going to return that child, Ms Hamble? Stealing the next generation from desperate families is one thing but when you already have progeny of your own, well, that's downright cruel.' Sean's eyes glinted maliciously at the sounds of disbelief that came from people sitting around the table.

Martha knew there was no point in defending her father or protesting that she'd known nothing about the sales. The entire city already knew the previous administration had been involved with the additional growth and sale of babies. It was the second horrific discovery her government had made after the water treatment. None of them had had any idea such practices had been occurring. Holding her dignity together, her voice barely shook as she acquiesced.

'Very well, an escort to my office would be acceptable.'

Martha turned and walked slowly back the way she had come, numb with disbelief. She thanked her foresight and the brilliance of Operative Ash that her entire system was backed up onto an independent drive that only she could access, from home. A backup system that she had never shared with Sean. He may think he had removed her from office, but he hadn't locked her out of her city, and she would do everything within her power to get to the bottom of whatever the frag was happening right now.

It took five minutes to empty out her office. She grabbed her fern, her Gaia statue and the few personal effects scattered about the room not even bothering to look at the computer or info grabs that scattered her desk.

The Corporation guard nodded towards the handheld Martha still gripped tightly.

'It's my personal one,' she replied crisply. He shrugged and stood to one side, allowing her to exit.

There was no-one around to watch Martha leave for

which she was extremely grateful. She held her head high, carrying her meagre effects, and signalled for a nearby city skimmer to take her home. She'd be damned if she was going to use one of the governor ones. For all she knew it would deliberately crash or whisk her away to prison.

C42N: Shocking Update - Martha Hamble deposed!
Who will run City 42 now?

ANON17: Clear out the trash, make way for
Corporation to return.

MSCHILD: What about the baby Hamble stole? Is she
going to get away with it?

SMAC: I can confirm the removal of Martha Hamble as
governor of City 42. More details to follow.

She knew she was experiencing some kind of detached shock. She couldn't actually feel anything, she felt numb. Her brain was still trying to process the mass murder Jed had reported from City 15 and now, now she had lost her position as City Governor. And no-one knew about the murders. No-one knew about City 15. Or did Sean already know? And was that security guard wearing a Corporation uniform? Was Corp back in City 42? What the hell was going on? As all these thoughts swirled around her head, she considered the possibility that City 15 and the whole expedition out there had been a set up for Jed. Sean could use the massacre as a reason to get rid of the Force militia, those loyal to the city and to her. No-one had any proof of what happened out there. It would be one man's word against another, and Sean clearly had the support of the board plus some serious backing if Corporation truly was back in City 42.

She had always known it would be a possibility that Corporation would try and retake control, but she had hoped she would've had the chance to talk to their representatives and work out some kind of feasible arrangement. She didn't think the changes her government had instigated had been arduous for the city, if anything she had tried to do everything within her power to help each and every citizen.

She was still mulling over her options when she got to the apartment she shared with Ruth. She could hear children crying from outside the front door and she suddenly felt like her son, and the others, were in grave danger. She rushed into the apartment and saw at once all three children were in an expanded play cube. They didn't appear to be harmed in any way, but Martha rushed to soothe them. Lucas soon quietened down after a hug from his mother but Sarah and the as yet, unnamed little one, were harder to pacify. Martha tried calling for Ruth but there was no answer. In desperation she activated the cartoon ring around the cube and quickly all three children were absorbed by the bright colours and shapes, the odd sniff being the only sign that they were ever in distress. Putting Lucas down, Martha checked her room first, but it was empty, so she went through to Ruth's and found her crumpled body on the floor.

Chapter 14

C42N: Who is fit to take over from Martha Hamble as Governor of City 42? Join the discussion in social hub beta.

SMAC: The additional security guards are here to keep you safe. A new Governor will be announced in due course.

ANON17: Good riddance to bad rubbish - let's bring Corporation back.

MED4C42: Diagnostic pods will remain closed. Supplies are still limited.

ACAD: All our courses will continue as normal. Students are expected to attend. Ruth Maddocks has stepped down.

FORCE: No comment.

'Ruth! Ruth - can you hear me? Oh frag, are you okay? What happened?' Martha ran to where her friend lay on the floor, face down, and crouched beside her. Martha shook her shoulder gently but there was no response. She tried to remember her basic medical training, but she couldn't gather her thoughts together coherently. She wasn't sure whether she was doing the right thing or not but she decided to roll Ruth over on her side so she could see her face. Ruth was still breathing but her eyes were closed. She groaned a little at the movement and a small bottle rolled out of her hand.

Martha picked up the bottle and read the label. Sleeping tablets? Why was Ruth taking these? They were out of date judging by the label and as she shook the bottle slightly, Martha realised there were still a few left. These must be left over from Ruth's dabbling in the black market she thought. Before becoming pregnant Ruth had still indulged in the old-fashioned habit of smoking but of course that all changed with the baby. Ruth hadn't wanted to do anything to endanger the miracle.

Was Ruth taking these tablets because of Sarah? Martha knew the baby cried a lot at night, but she couldn't understand why Ruth had taken some now, during the daytime. Then the realisation hit her. Ruth had tried to take her own life. Tears pricked Martha's eyes, she felt awful - how could she have missed her friend's despair? Then Martha felt angry, Ruth could have endangered her son. It wasn't like Ruth to be self-involved; she had always put their babies first and had seemed happy to take on the childcare but clearly the arrangement wasn't working.

Fresh wails came from the children in the front room. Martha grabbed her handheld from her pocket, embarrassed to have only thought of this now.

'Run a basic health scan,' she ordered and then let out a relieved breath when everything came back within normal parameters. It looked like Ruth hadn't taken enough tablets to cause any permanent damage. Instead, she would have a good night's sleep for once.

Hurrying back to the children, Martha rang the only person she could think of who would be able to help at a moment's notice. Kira's mum.

'Thank you so much for coming, Jean.' Martha answered the door with Lucas on one hip and Sarah on the other leaving the third child sniffling in the play cube. She tried to smile but her bottom lip wobbled.

'Oh Martha, my dear. I can see we've got ourselves into a bit of a pickle here. You've got your hands full and no mistake. Not to worry, love. I'm here now and we'll get everything in order. I've brought along Malcolm with some bits and pieces, so I'll stay with you tonight. He can help us with Ruth. Here, give me Sarah.' And she held her arms out for the little girl who went willingly.

Jean took charge, ushering Martha to the sofa and tucking her son into her arms so they could comfort each other. She motioned for them to stay where they were as she went through to check on Ruth, her husband in tow, Sarah still being cuddled.

Martha felt herself calming down, helped by the peaceful slumbering of her son. He had quietened as well, thanks to being held by his mummy. Thinking about that connection bought tears to her eyes as she watched the other little boy in the play cube who would never know his parents.

There were some muffled noises and a loud grunt from Ruth's room then Jean and Malcolm both came back through, Jean pulling the door close so as not to disturb Ruth. She caught Martha's eye and smiled.

'I expect she'd sleep through a fire alarm but just in case. Snoring like a bear she is. It's best she gets her rest.'

Malcolm walked over to Martha and gave her hand a brief squeeze. 'Bad business, love. Try not to worry, we'll get through.'

She struggled to blink away the tears. She'd always liked Kira's dad, but it was when he spoke to her like this that she really missed her own, gruff father. She watched as Jean directed her husband to set up two sleeping cubes in the front room whilst she busied herself making up three bottles and some synth-caf. She somehow managed to entertain Sarah and unpack the bags she'd brought with her at the same time.

There were little packages of dried biscuits, some desiccated fruit, nuts and best of all, a tin with some freshly baked biscuits. Despite the food issues City 42 had been having, somehow Jean never missed the opportunity to bake and bring a little something round when she visited. When it was ready, Jean brought the synth-caf over to Martha and a bottle for Lucas when he woke, then nestled Sarah and two more bottles in the other sofa before going to pick up the new baby.

'So, who's this extra little one then?' she asked as she sat down with a baby either side, deftly feeding them both their milk. She waited patiently for Martha to answer, checking on the children and sipping her synth-caf, seeming to have an extra pair of hands as she dealt with burps, dribbles and managing not to spill her own drink. When they'd finished, Jean snuggled both children sleepily into the opposite corners of the sofa and hemmed them in with cushions, letting them fall sleep.

Martha looked down at her son. She cleared her throat, trying to think of how to tell Jean who the extra child was.

'Oh, Jean. Where to start? The baby - it's Pete and Ingrid's. I don't know how he survived but we ran a DNA test to confirm it. I don't even think he has a name,' Martha said, close to tears. 'And then I found out Ruth has stepped down from Academy, but I didn't know she was struggling, she never said a thing. I came home, found her like that and... and... rang you.'

'Have you told Jed yet? Or his parents?' Jean asked.

Martha shook her head, horrified that she hadn't yet thought about contacting Jed or his parents, Gretchen and Henry Jenkins.

'Right then.' Jean extracted herself out of the sofa and put her cup down. 'I'll talk to Gretchen; she can be a bit prickly at the best of times. Probably best if I break this news rather than you. I see you've had a lot of sweeps today.' Jean waited expectantly for Martha to deny the obvious rumours that were flying over the sweeps but when she didn't speak and looked at Jean in mute appeal, she tutted to herself. 'Well, well, well. They finally took some action. I can't say I'm surprised. I always thought Corporation gave up too easy. That's not to say you haven't done a fine job my dear, a fine job, but they weren't about to loosen their claws from our city. That's for sure. Well, what will be will be I suppose, we'll have to ride it out whichever way it goes. But don't worry, my love, me and Malcolm will make sure nothing happens to you or the children. Do you want me to see to Lucas as well, love?' Jean asked gently.

Martha shook her head to clear the fuzziness. 'No, it's okay. I'll do it. But I think I'll turn in as well. Do you need me to do anything?'

'No dear, it's all under control. But, do you know

when Kira and Jed will be back?'

'No, not yet. They're coming back from City 15 now. They should check in when they get back to Camp Eden. Should I stay up for that, do you think?' Martha dithered, not knowing what to do for the best.

Jean pushed her gently in the direction of her room. 'You go get some rest. Take your handheld, that way you'll hear the comms and if it comes in here, I'll come get you. We'll tell him, don't worry, dear.'

Martha nodded gratefully and let herself be ushered into her room. It was blissfully dark and quiet. She lay Lucas in his cube and without bothering to undress, fell into her own bed and was asleep within minutes.

Jean poked her head into Martha's room and nodded with satisfaction. Then she squared her shoulders, about to make a terribly difficult phone call to Jed's mother. She hoped the woman wouldn't ask too many questions because she had no answers to give.

'Gretchen? It's Jean. Jean Bishop.'

'Yes, hello? It's rather late for a social call, isn't it?'

'There's something important you should know.'

'I already do. That silly young girl got herself more than she bargained for and has been voted out of office. Just because she was Hamble's daughter, doesn't mean she was the right person for the job.'

'Hmm, that's not what I wanted to talk to you about.'

'Where are you? Are you at her apartment? Is Jed there? That boy has been avoiding my pings. I don't want him caught up in any kind of scandal.' Gretchen patted her perfectly coiffed hair. 'He does have a career ahead of him, you know.'

'Jed's not here, but I do need to speak to you.'

Gretchen leaned in closer to the vid comm. 'Is it true that Martha stole a baby from the growth lab?'

Jean sighed. 'It's your grandson.'

'I beg your pardon.' Gretchen's face had gone white, her lips pinched, eyes round. 'Is this your idea of some kind of dreadful prank?'

'No.' For once Jean Bishop was at a loss of what to say, so she stayed quiet.

Gretchen's nostrils flared wildly as she controlled her grief and anger, then she abruptly cut the link.

'You'd better put on another pot of synth-caf, love,' Jean said to her husband. 'I think we'll have some visitors soon.'

ANON40: Lots of people visiting Hamble's apartment - how much longer does she get to stay there?

C42N: Both Kira & Jed Jenkins' parents have visited Martha Hamble's apartment. Did something terrible happen in City 15? Sweep what you know!

Chapter 15

'Can we stop at Camp Eden?' asked Kira. She was still feeling nauseous at the thought of the deaths they had seen and the cremation they'd performed. She wanted to replenish her spirit by spending some time in the lush green of the science camp, revisit the orchards and tune in to nature. If she was lucky enough, she'd get to see Gaia again, too. It seemed like the most obvious place to try. There wasn't much nature to be found in City 42, yet.

'Yes, love. I want to reconnect to the sweeps, get a handle on what's been happening while we were away, before we get back to the city,' Jed replied.

'Why? What did Martha say?'

'It's not what she said, it's how she looked. Something's going on.'

Kira laughed softly. 'Don't forget she's got two babies keeping her awake on top of running an entire city. Do you remember how tired we used to get?'

They both looked fondly at Grace who was staring out of the skimmer window, cooing and gurgling at unseen magic.

It didn't take long to get to Camp Eden. Both skimmers were fully charged, and everyone wanted to get as far away from City 15 as quickly as possible. The camp was, as always, a place of peace and tranquillity. Moham was at hand to greet them all. The operatives sloped off to the mess tent, eager to get a hot meal while the others, including Ash, congregated in the relaxation area. Moham bought over real tea and some fresh fruit for them. Kira felt so relaxed that for a moment, she wished they could forget everything else and live here, in this peace, forever.

'Are those new, Moham?' Kira pointed to the beehives that nestled in the far corner of the camp, near the orchard.

'Yes, we have been fortunate - a queen has taken up residence in the first hive so it shouldn't be long before we have honey to share,' replied Moham, grinning.

'That's wonderful. Any sightings?' She didn't have to be specific, Moham knew she meant Gaia. He shook his head sadly.

'Aha!' exclaimed Ash, making everyone jump. 'Sorry. Finally got connected to the Sweeps.'

They all opened their handhelds and began to check their messages and most importantly the newsfeed. Then everyone started talking at once.

'Martha's been removed from office?'

'She stole a baby? That can't be right.'

'Corporation are back in City 42? What the frag happened in the last two days?'

Kira, Dina and Jed were all trying to talk over each other, shouting louder and louder to make themselves be heard.

'HEY! ENOUGH!' Max's shout startled Grace so much, she began to cry. Kira shot him a wounded look. 'I'm sorry but we won't get to the bottom of anything with you lot shouting over each other. We've all got

113

different top news stories so let's share what we have and try to sift the fact from the fiction. Alright?'

There was a bit of grumbling, but the others knew Max was right.

'Who goes first?' asked Kira.

'Why don't you start? Read your private messages first.' Max replied, then turned to his left. 'Ash, can you keep track of it all please?'

Ash nodded.

'Okay. Personal messages - I've got one from my mum, well several actually. Hoping we're alright, asking about the meds - she's running low.' Kira paused to try and stop tears from overcoming her. 'She says something awful has happened to Ma... wait, and to Ruth. That was her last message.' Kira frantically scrolled. 'I don't have anything from either of those two though.'

Dina shook her head, 'Me either, I've got nothing useful in personal. Jed?'

Jed looked grave. 'I have an emergency message from Martha on a private channel. It's not good news. She's been ousted as governor. Corporation security guards were in place at Hamble HQ and it seems Sean MacIntyre has taken over, in the interim. Nothing about Ruth.'

'What do we do? We should get back there - it has to be some kind of mistake, doesn't it?' Dina pleaded, looking at the others for reassurance.

'We stay put. Martha says to contact her as soon as we can.' Jed turned to Ash. 'You set up her backup system, didn't you? Can you get me access, see if we can't get a decent comms link established? Off the main network?'

'Of course.' Ash nodded and let Max lead him over to the tech centre of the camp. Everything was fairly high-end so it wouldn't be too difficult to establish a secure connection.

'Kira, reply to your Mum. Let her know we're all okay but keep it vague. Ask her to wait before sending anymore messages. We don't want too much chatter on an open channel,' Jed said and Kira began tapping away, trying to sound light and airy in her message when inside she was panicking.

'Dina, what sweeps have you got? Dina!'

Dina jumped; she'd been miles away.

'Um, I don't... what?'

'Sweeps. What are your top sweeps?' asked Jed.

'Right.' Dina looked down at her handheld and started reading.

C42N: Do we want Sean MacIntyre in charge? Do you think someone else would be a better fit? Do you agree with Hamble's ejection? Join the discussion in social hub beta.

ANON17: Don't bother coming back, Jenkins. City 42 needs no protector but Corporation.

SMAC: I have the best interests of City 42 at the heart of everything I do. Bringing back Corporation will help everyone. More supplies - more tech - safety.

ACAD: We remain open to students. New leadership to be determined.

ANON17: GOVHAM stole a baby! Why hasn't she returned him?

C42N: Hamble is not returning the baby. Sweep your

views.

ANON40: *When will we actually start getting fresh supplies? So far nothing has changed.*

CORPTECH2: *Finally! With Corp back we will be able to rebuild and bring you the latest tech.*

MSCHILD: *Why hasn't SMAC confirmed the reopening of the baby labs? I want my collection! Tell Hamble to bring back that baby!*

MED4C42: *We still do not have any new medical supplies. We are NOT turning diagnostic pods back on.*

Dina finished reading. 'ANON17 is such a dick, Jed. Ignore him,' she said.

'Don't worry, Dina. I've had worse. Your top sweeps pretty much match what I've got as well. No real difference. None of it makes any sense though,' Jed replied. 'It looks like Sean doesn't have the whole city convinced although there's more Corporation support than I expected. And why would Martha steal a baby from the lab?'

'She must have had a good reason. There's no way Ruth would want another one in their flat,' replied Dina.

'I know what you mean. Has she said anything to you?' Kira asked in concern.

Dina shifted uncomfortably. 'Well... I know she's not been coping too well. Feeling tired, super emotional, like she doesn't know what she's doing or what's the best way to do things. You know, that sort of thing.'

'But she won't ask us for help so what are we supposed to do?' Kira felt sad. Surely, she would have

116

been the perfect person for Ruth to talk to. She'd recently gone through the same thing Ruth was going through. Well, mostly. Apart from the birth. And Ruth had had Martha to support her through that. It had all gone well at the med centre, despite everyone involved having to use centuries old resources from Archive to ensure best practice and the highest level of care. But it had all gone fine. And Sarah was such a lovely baby. As was Lucas.

'Look, I don't know why she hasn't said anything. Have you asked her how she's feeling? Maybe she doesn't want to bother you.' Dina shrugged. 'I thought they were going to get some help, you know, what with Martha working so hard and being away from Lucas - which I know she doesn't enjoy very much either. They were talking about your NanNan.' Dina faltered and looked at Jed.

'It doesn't work,' he replied gruffly and stood up, leaving the two women to their conversation.

'He doesn't mean anything by it, Dina.' Kira watched her husband walk away, feeling once again his pain at having lost his sister and best friend.

'Do you think Ruth and Martha are alright?' asked Dina.

'If I know Ash, we will have a secure comms connection with them soon and we'll be able to find out for ourselves. Let's try not to worry.' Kira turned her attention to her daughter and tried to quieten the feeling of dread building in the pit of her stomach.

Ash hurried over with a larger comms screen than the usual handheld. 'Here, use this portable. It's got a faster uplink.'

'And this will be secure? Martha and no-one else?' asked Jed as he took the device.

'It's as secure as I can manage. Provided no-one

117

suspects Martha of having a backdoor system, we should be fine. If Corporation have only moved back into the city, it will take them a while to sift through everything. Even they don't have unlimited resources.' He paused, considered what he'd witnessed in the past few days. 'Do they?'

Jed said nothing. Instead he pinged Martha. Kira and Dina came to join him, and everyone held their breath waiting to see if she would answer the call.

'Hello? Jed, is that you?'

'Yes, Martha. It's me. Are you alright? Can you talk?'

'Yes, yes I can talk. Let me try and improved the screen resolution.' The vid screen went black then fuzzy and then a clear image swam into view. Martha looked pale, red-eyed yet the sight of seeing her friends, her family, seemed to bolster her. She gave a brief smile in greeting, then began to speak.

'After you checked in with your mission report, Jed, I was alerted to an emergency board meeting that had been called in my absence. At first, I thought it was the meeting I was meant to brief everyone about the results of your expedition however it turned out to be something else entirely. It appears Sean MacIntyre has been building a base of support with those still loyal to Corporation and those dissatisfied with my governance. A call of no-confidence was issued, and I have been removed from office.'

There was silence from the team at Camp Eden as Martha confirmed the sweeps. They all sensed there was more to come.

'I can confirm that a Corporation security officer escorted me from the premises. I do not know how long there has been a Corp presence in the city. It could have been a spare uniform dug out to inspire confidence. I believe Sean and the rest of them are too short-sighted to see how dangerous it is to invite Corporation back into the city without any kind of accord drawn up. I think we have to assume that Sean is a Corper, through and through.'

There was murmured ascent through the group watching.

'Have you seen the sweeps?'

Kira nodded and then realised that Martha might not be able to see her on the edge of the vid comm screen. 'We've seen the sweeps,' she said. 'Or some of them anyway. Martha - they're accusing you of stealing a child.'

'I know.'

'Well... did you?'

'Of course not.' She paused. 'Technically yes, but I had good reason.' Martha turned to focus directly on Jed. 'I found Pete and Ingrid's child.'

The colour drained from Jed's face and he would've dropped the vid comm if Ash hadn't reacted quickly and caught it. There was a scrambled moment of connection as the link dipped and then re-established itself. Kira tried to get Jed's attention to see if he was alright, but he appeared unresponsive. Dina tugged her sleeve.

'Can you believe this?' she whispered.

Kira shook her head in bewilderment. This was huge. The baby survived. Somehow survived. And had been left in the growth lab all this time. Why didn't anybody know?

'How do you know?' Jed's voice sounded wooden, unemotional.

'We opened your NanNan and ran a DNA test. I accessed your personal records. I apologise but I needed

119

to be sure.'

Jed cocked his head to one side, unable to process the information. After a moment he shook his head. 'I just need...' he began to speak but faltered and walked away. Kira took a half step after him but stopped, unsure if she should intrude.

'I'll go with him,' Max said and followed Jed who stumbled a little in his shock. Kira moved closer to the comms screen.

'Who else knows about this, Ma?' she asked.

'Ruth and your mother. I needed some help here.'

'Of course - three children...' but before Kira could finish Martha interrupted her.

'It's not just that. Kira... Ruth... she took an overdose.' Martha's voice broke as she spoke the words.

'She didn't?' whispered Dina.

'Is she... did she...?' Kira couldn't bring herself to ask.

'She's fine. Well, no, she's not fine. She's a mess but she is alive. I want to send her, your parents and the children out to Camp Eden. I need you to stay there, for your safety but also to keep you out of whatever is happening here in the city. It's not safe for us - again. I don't want to put anyone at risk.'

'What about you?' Dina realised Martha hadn't included herself in that plan. 'Are you intending to stay in the city? They're going to crucify you for everything that has gone wrong, is going wrong. That's not fair!'

'They're going to do that anyway, Dina. At least this way I can try and gather some loyal supporters and protect the rights of the citizens of City 42 as best I can.'

'But Martha...'

'It's okay. I'm counting on you to find us the help we need.'

'Me?'

'All of you. Kira, you still have plans for the nearest cities in the area, don't you?' asked Martha.

'Yes. But why...?' Kira frowned then answered her own question. 'Oh, you want us to try and establish contact somewhere else.'

'Yes, I do. And this is where I think you should go,' said Martha as she outlined her plan.

Chapter 16

'Jed, are you alright?'

Kira had gone to find her husband. She smiled gratefully at Max who dipped his head and went back to Dina and the last of the hot tea.

'Jed?' Kira called his name again.

He turned his face to look at her.

'Can you believe it? I mean, it's something I hoped for. I could never accept that the doctors would terminate a new life like that. It felt so wrong. Something that even Corporation couldn't do. And I was right. I was right, Kira. My nephew - he's alive!' Jed smiled crookedly at her. He was obviously still fighting the grief of losing his sister and best friend but now at least he had some family back. He clutched her arm. 'Do you think he can, I mean, would he... should he come and live with us? Do you think?'

Kira shook her head, unsure. 'I don't know, love. I don't know who the legal guardian would be. It might be your mother.'

'Oh, no.' Jed shook his head. 'Oh no, no, no. She can't raise him. She doesn't raise children well.'

'She didn't do such a bad job with you.'

Jed barked a laugh and then went for his handheld. 'I

have to talk to her.'

Kira stopped him. 'You can't, love. Not yet. We need you to come back to the conversation, Martha has some ideas. You need to listen.'

Jed looked at her, not understanding at first and then remembering everything that had happened. It was difficult to focus, he still felt giddy at the good news. 'Right. Yes. What happens next. Of course. Come on, then.' He took his wife's hand and together they walked back to the others.

'Jed.' Martha sounded relieved when she saw him. 'Are you alright?'

He nodded. 'Can we see him? My nephew?'

Martha shook her head.

'He's asleep I'm afraid and you probably ought to speak to your mother. She's not happy about the current situation,' Martha said. 'I'm trying to find out the legal standpoint but nothing like this has ever happened before and I only have access to limited resources.'

'I want him with us. With Kira and me and Grace. I'll deal with my mother.' Jed was emphatic.

'Okay. Good. Now, listen. This is what I think we should do. I will send the children, Kira's parents and Ruth out to you guys at Camp Eden. Max, is the camp secure? I mean, do you have the resources to keep the children safe?' Martha asked.

Max ran his hands through his hair. 'Well, we have enough space and we can feed them no problem. But this isn't a military camp, Martha. We don't have weapons or anything like that.'

'No, I didn't think you would have. Jed, I've been in touch with Chief Minkov. He is sending out the rest of your militia team, fully equipped with all their gear and vehicles.'

Kira interrupted. 'Won't that leave the city exposed?'

'Corporation are already here, Kira. Besides the chief feels the rest of the Force operatives he has are still loyal to the shield and will do their best to protect citizen rights. They have their own riot gear and supplies. We will keep the citizens safe.'

'You're definitely not coming?' asked Jed.

'I need to stay here. If nothing else I need to keep attention away from you and try to prevent Corporation dismantling everything we've worked so hard to achieve. I still have friends. I won't be alone.' She leaned into the vidcom. 'Look after Lucas, won't you?'

'Ma! Of course we will and we'll all see each other soon.' Kira replied, eyes shining.

'What's our next move?' Jed asked. 'I assume you are not sending the rest of my team out here to sit on our hands?'

'No. I want you to try and make contact with another city.'

'Which one?' Jed was intrigued.

'As I told the others, I've been thinking about that,' said Martha. 'We should probably split our focus and send one team to City 9 by the coast. I know it's a Corporation stronghold, but they may have access to additional transportation and information about what's beyond our country. If we've started to heal, there's a chance the rest of the world has too. We can then send a second team into the mountains to find City 36. Corporation might not be that far north.'

'What about what happened in City 15?' asked Jed.

'We can't let that stop us from finding out more information. We need to know if Corporation rules everywhere in our country and whether they have a presence abroad. We need to know for sure who was behind City 15. We can't let the death of all those people be in vain. The rest of the cities - if they still exist - have to know that this kind of corruption cannot be allowed to rule our lives, and our children's lives. We have to try.' Martha waited to see what her friends would say.

Jed nodded in agreement. 'I'll wait until the rest of my team gets here and then we'll decide who goes where. Are your comms secure?'

'They are for now. Ash and I set up an enclosed comms ring a while back. It should be untraceable.'

'Who do you have to help you, Martha?' Kira asked in concern.

'Ben is dropping by.'

'Ben? I don't think that's a good idea,' said Jed.

'You may be right, Jed, but at the very least he knows how to stay under the radar and that is something we all need to do. Look, I have to go, the children...' Martha looked away from the console for a moment. 'They'll be with you tomorrow morning. Take good care of them.' And she signed off, not letting anyone respond to her final words.

The group drifted away to chat amongst themselves and digest the news leaving Kira and Jed alone.

'I'd better sort out the operatives. Are you alright with Grace?' Jed asked.

'Yes, I can manage. Come and find me when you're done.' Kira gave him a quick kiss and took Grace back to the cohabitation tent. She had just put Grace down for the night when the others came back and made themselves comfortable on the other side of the sleeping area. Jed's team had decided to make camp on the other side of the clearing and use their pods, so it wasn't too crowded in the tent.

'Kira? You all done?' Jed asked quietly.

She nodded and came with him to sit with the rest of them, casting a quick glance back at Grace's cube. The baby was already fast asleep.

'We need to know about these two cities Martha wants us to try and communicate with. Did you happen to download the details before you left 42?' Jed asked his wife.

'Of course I did. I can forward the full files over to your handhelds, but I can give you a brief outline now if you like.'

'Yes please.'

'City 9 is based on the southern coastline of the country. It's where a lot of trade and travel used to occur, before The Event I mean, so the infrastructure for water transport should still be available.'

'Will there be boats?' Dina's eyes sparkled in excitement.

'I don't know, maybe. But the real problem will be finding someone who knows how to operate them. It's one of the lost skills unfortunately. Anyway, City 9 have, or had, different technology to us, they were originally working on cleaning the seawater - I don't know how badly the HER weapons affected the ocean. Or to what extent marine life was afflicted. The rising sea temperatures have of course changed the entire ecosystem. It's mainly jellyfish in that region, or at least it was.'

'Jellyfish eh, bet they make you feel wobbly,' joked Max.

Dina poked him in the arm as the others rolled their eyes. 'I think they are edible,' she said. 'If prepared correctly. It's something else to try, I guess.' However breezy she sounded Dina didn't look convinced.

'What do we know about the Corporation presence

in City 9?' Jed asked.

'It's a Corp controlled city so I expect they will be everywhere. From the reports Archive had, City 9 has more tech than we do but otherwise standard Corporation stuff. I'd be surprised if Corporation didn't have all the coastal regions under their control to be honest. One thing we can hope is that they haven't treated their water supply the way they did in 42. We might see natural reproduction in action.'

There was a brief silence as the group digested the information Kira shared.

'What about 36 then, up in the mountains?' asked Max.

'That is in completely the other direction. If you consider the entire map of our island, the two cities couldn't be further apart. It will take us at least a day and a half to travel up there. Not knowing what the travel routes are like, of course.'

'It seems like it's in the middle of nowhere,' Dina commented as she looked at the map on her handheld. 'Why would they establish a city up there?'

'It sort of is but that could work well in our favour,' replied Kira. 'The citizens of 36 are more likely to be self-reliant and I think there's a greater chance for them to be out from under the rule of Corporation. It would have been difficult to resupply up there initially, so their technology is either state of the art or incredibly basic. They might have rediscovered some of the old trades and industries. It's definitely where I'd go if I was looking for a safe place away from Corporation. I think 9 puts us close to potential trade routes which, let's face it, Corporation will be all over.'

'Oh, I wanted to see the jellyfish,' Dina said wistfully.

'Kira, make sure you send everyone the full reports for both cities, please.' Jed looked around at the group. 'I want everyone to have read them by tomorrow morning. I think the best thing to do is to split into teams and cover both our bases, but I want to make sure we have all the facts before we make any kind of decisions.'

Kira nodded and began tapping out instructions on her handheld. It wouldn't take long to transfer the info parcels to the others.

Later that evening, when everyone was absorbed in reading about cities 9 and 36, Kira discussed Jed's idea with him.

'Do you really think we should split up? After what we saw in 15? Surely safety in numbers is the way to go.'

'I think we need answers and fast,' replied Jed. 'If the chief is sending the rest of my team out here then we will have ample numbers of operatives to run two missions plus extra skimmers and supplies. We ought to try and get as much intel as possible. And splitting up our expertise base makes sense as well.' He smiled at his wife. 'It seems pointless to send an experienced anthropologist such as yourself to a seaport to eat jellyfish and two biologists up to the mountains to carry out research on what may be a tribe of people adapted to a completely different way of life.'

Kira gave him a huge hug. 'Then we are going to 36?'

'More than likely, love. More than likely.' Jed paused. 'Look, if your parents are coming here, will you leave Grace with them so she can stay here, at Camp Eden?'

Kira frowned and glanced at the nearby cube. 'I don't know. We could be gone a week or longer. My gut says she'll be safer if she's with us. And Jed, don't forget, Mum's not well. She can't have much medication left.' Her voice changed, becoming urgent and low. 'We should take her with us, use her condition as a bargaining chip for medication.'

'Yes, but, if it's Corporation medication we're after, she may be better off travelling to 9 with Dina and Max.'

Kira was silent.

'Hey, don't worry, everything will work out - you'll see. We'll find some meds for your mum, and a safe place for the children, and us, to live.' He checked his wristplant. 'It's getting late, we'd better get some rest. Everyone will be here in the morning and I need to report to Martha first thing with our plan.'

Kira nodded, hugged her husband and went to curl up on the camp bed, next to Grace's cube. She didn't think she would be able to sleep a wink but within minutes she had drifted away, imagining what the people of 36 would be like and whether they'd share their way of life with the rest of them.

Jed was pleased. It seemed to him that a workable plan was beginning to come together. It was a shame to have to split everyone up, but it made sense to send the expertise where it could be used effectively. Max and Dina would be alright. If 9 was all Corper, they'd be able to blend in, more or less, and their scientific skills might even gain them access to whatever research or plans Corporation was working on. The more he thought about it, the more Jed realised that they had no idea whether Corporation was a worldwide entity or whether it just held sway on their island. Travelling to a coastal city would more than likely provide that information. Or at least a few clues to what lay beyond the ocean.

Corporation had taught them that there had been

fifty cities established around the globe after The Event. Cities where the remains of the human population had been sent to survive and re-establish themselves but after everything that had happened recently, Jed had a hard time believing that to be the whole truth. What if there were competing organisations? What if there were more people, more cities? More soberly, what if there were less? Jed couldn't believe that 42 was it, now that 15 was gone. Half of him hoped that they never came up against the power behind that mass execution whilst the other half was desperate to fight back in retaliation. No-one should have that kind of power or think they had the justification to wipe out a city on a whim. No-one.

Chapter 17

C42N: What will Hamble do now? Join the conversation in social hub beta.

FORCE: We are merging with Corp Security. The safety of City 42 citizens is paramount.

ANON17: Why isn't the team back from City 15 yet? What are they trying to hide?

GJENK: Hamble did not 'snatch' the baby-lab child. It is my grandson. My son will become legal guardian.

MSCHILD: How do we know GJENK is telling the truth? That baby died in Corp Tech tragedy.

CORPTECH2: We are thrilled to hear of another survivor.

SMAC: The Governor Office can confirm the child in the baby-lab did belong to Ingrid Jenkins and Pete Barnes. We extend our sympathies for the mix-up in placement.

Martha was trying to pack. She knew that Lucas was going to be in safe hands, but her heart hurt at the thought of sending him away.

'Am I doing the right thing?' She asked Jean as she tried to fold clothes and not bawl her eyes out.

'Martha, my lovely, come on. Don't get yourself into such a state. You don't have to do this you know, love. You could just leave them all to it. There's no reason for you to stay here.' Jean rubbed Martha gently on the back.

'I have to. I promised my Father I would look after the citizens of City 42.' Martha turned to look at Jean. 'I haven't done a very good job so far, have I?'

'You did an excellent job. You uncovered the water treatment and you found us a safe, clean alternative. You sorted out all that mess after Corp Tech was destroyed. You even found the little boy - who we need a name for by the way. We can't keep calling him the boy. Have you had any thoughts?'

'I'm not sure it's my place...'

'Peter, I think we should call him Peter,' Jean interrupted. 'I'll tell Gretchen. I see she swept about it - good of her. I'm surprised she hasn't decided she's coming with us, but her lot are all tied into Corporation and if they're back in town then she'll do well out of it I expect.'

'She knows we're going to Camp Eden?'

'Not as such, but she's knows we're going to go meet Jed, introduce him to his nephew. I had to say something, love. She was hell bent on taking that child, Peter, with her when she left. If I hadn't had my Malcolm to back me up, I dread to think what would've happened.'

Martha couldn't help smiling at that. Jean was a dynamo, a real force of nature, whereas Kira's dad was one of the gentlest, softly spoken men she'd ever come across.

'Now look, you listen to me. I say you come with us. Think about the realities here, Martha. You're a young girl, a young mother for goodness sake. It won't do your Lucas any good to be away from you for an extended period of time. I mean, did you hear about that girl over on 7th? She left her one with the NanNan exclusively so she could carry on gadding about like a mad thing and in the end the child wanted nothing to do with her. They emancipated themselves. Do you remember that? How that girl ever got a baby from the lottery I'll never know but I guess that was Corporation for you.'

Martha hadn't heard that one but there were plenty of stories like it. People who were so ill-equipped for the role of parenthood that they relied too heavily on the available tech and their children were total corpers and tech heads.

It all works in Corporations' favour she thought. She couldn't imagine Lucas growing up without her. Martha picked up a jumpsuit and began refolding it for the tenth time. Should she stay and be the voice for the people? She felt confused, the more she considered Jean's words, the more she realised that her son had to come first.

'Besides, we need you to help Ruth out of this black hole she's got herself into. She'll listen to you,' remarked Jean.

'I'm not sure about that,' replied Martha, guilt flickering in her stomach. 'I didn't even know she was struggling. And she hasn't been told about City 15 yet. How is she going to react to that?'

'I don't know, love. But she needs to be told. She can't keep ignoring Sarah forever, especially now the little one will never meet her father. We've got to surround Ruth with love and help her through whatever it is she's struggling with, that's all there is to it.'

Martha put down the clothes she had been folding and unfolding.

'You're absolutely right, Jean. Lucas needs me and so does Ruth. There's nothing I can do here, apart from become the target practice for everything Corporation want to blame on me. It's clear they intend to take back the city and if all my family have left then I'm only staying to be a martyr.'

'Your father wouldn't have wanted that for you, love. He sent you to Eden before, didn't he?'

Martha nodded, thinking fondly of her father's gruffness. The door pinged, surprising both women.

'Are you expecting anyone, dear?' asked Jean.

'I don't think so... oh, it's probably Ben.' Martha hurried to key open the door. Sure enough, Jed's cousin Ben sauntered into the flat. He grinned widely when he saw Jean, she was his Aunty by marriage and much loved.

'Lo, Auntie. I didn't know you'd be here. I brought these for Kira to pass on to you.' He reached round to the satchel slung across his body and took out a large bag of medical supplies.

Jean held out a hand for the bag and looked inside. For once she was lost for words. She crushed the bag shut and pressed it to her chest, smiling at Ben, eyes shining brightly.

'What is it?' asked Martha.

'Auntie's medicine. Or at least as much as I could find. I figured once you lot get out to Eden the scientists out there might be able to replicate it or something.'

'That's so good of you, Ben. Thank you.'

'Well, I got to look after my family, right? I hear

you've been busy, Martha. Stealing babies, upsetting things.'

Martha replied hotly. 'I did NOT steal a baby. I'll have you know that Peter belongs with us and I am only bringing him to his real family.' Then she flushed as she realised Ben was teasing her. 'Do you want to meet him? I think he must be a second cousin or something to you.'

Ben nodded and followed Martha over to the play cube where the three little ones were happily playing together.

'He looks like Pete, don't he?' Ben said softly. 'Except for them eyes, those are Ingrid's eyes.' He sniffed rather loudly then reached into his satchel again pulling out a couple of handhelds. 'These are for you. They're encrypted so they won't show up on Corp's radar but use them sparingly to get in touch with me. I'm being watched.' He jerked a head towards the pile of packed bags. 'You going too?'

Martha nodded. 'Why don't you come with us?'

'To the middle of the jungle with a load of rug-rats? Not my style, Martha. Besides you might need an inside man.'

'You will be careful, won't you?'

'Model citizen I am, they got nothing on me. Besides, working for Chief Minkov now, ain't I? I got a bit of muscle behind me if anything goes wrong.'

That was a surprise to Martha, she had always thought the chief had little or no time for Ben after he had been exposed as an active Anti-Corp member in the wake of the terrorist attack on Corp Tech. Clearly the two men had moved on. However, Force was now out of favour as well.

'Watch out for Corporation, Ben. They're after Minkov too. We'll be in touch; let you know how we get on. You can always come and join us later, if you want to?'

He nodded, looked like he was going to hug her then decided against it. Instead he planted a kiss on his Auntie's cheek and called out a goodbye to everyone.

Martha watched him leave then gave herself a little shake. She needed to pack the rest of her things now, Jean was right. She couldn't do anything here; she'd tried her best. What she needed to do was find a safe place for herself, her child and her friends. She tried to ignore the growing fear that whatever had wiped out City 15 was coming for them next.

Ruth sat motionless in her room. There was hustle and bustle around her as Kira's mum packed up her life for her. She watched dispassionately. There wasn't much here anyway. Mostly baby things and most of those had been Martha getting over excited and buying two of everything. Sarah was in the front room. Ruth knew she should feel a twinge of guilt over abandoning the children's care the other day, but she didn't feel anything. Apart from empty. She couldn't see the point in travelling out to Camp Eden. If Corporation had returned to the city, it wouldn't take them long to travel out to Eden and bring everyone back under control. Living under their regime would be simpler. She could pass Sarah off to a NanNan and get some faceless job somewhere. Jacking in whenever she wanted any kind of distraction and keeping her friends virtual. Then she wouldn't have to hear people whispering or catch their looks of pity.

Anger stirred in the pit of her stomach momentarily, but her apathy took over. There wasn't any point. Ruth realised that Jean was stood in front of her, holding things in her hands.

'Whatever you think is best, Jean. I don't care.' And with that Ruth lay down and rolled over, her back to the room and to the lady who was trying to help. Jean tutted and went to find Martha.

'We need to do something about that girl, Martha. She's not coping well. I think we ought to keep Sarah safely away for now; although maybe that's the worst thing to do. I wonder if we should put the two of them together in a room and see what happens. I can't say I can abide a baby crying at all hours. There's no need for that. Not when we have so many hands available. It costs nothing for a hug, and it does you the world of good.'

Martha let Jean ramble on. She was worried about Ruth and felt intensely guilty that she hadn't noticed the signs prior to Ruth's suicide attempt. A change of scenery might do her some good. Perhaps Gaia would visit her out in Camp Eden. City 42 didn't feel like a very spiritual place at the moment. The sweeps were full of derogatory comments aimed at Martha and the people who had supported her in office, which included Ruth. A lot of those people had also stepped down. What kind of lives would they now live? Martha supposed the most politically agile would hang on to the coat tails of the next rising star, which seemed to be Sean.

Gretchen had at least smoothed over the baby-snatching by sweeping that the child was her grandson and he would be going into care with Kira and Jed. There was surprisingly little commentary on the revelation that the baby belonged to Ingrid, that his apparent death had been the spark that began the revolution. Martha supposed that was because Corporation were extending their influence over the sweeps again. The whole business exhausted her. Now that she'd made the decision to leave, she just wanted to

137

leave.

The door pinged. It was a member of the City Guard, one of Jed's operatives he'd left behind and who would be travelling with them to Camp Eden. 'The skimmer is ready for you, Ma'am er, Ms Hamble.'

'Thank you. We'll be down shortly.' She smiled at the young woman and went to get the children. With Martha carrying Lucas and Sarah, Jean took Peter and Malcolm piled all the bags onto a hover transport to take them down to the skimmer. It just remained to get Ruth moving and out of the door.

Jean had finished packing for Ruth and was busy directing her husband in the best way to stack the various bags. Martha shook Ruth's shoulder as she lay on the bed, facing away from the room.

'It's time to go.'

There was no response.

'Ruth, come on. It's time to leave. You don't have to do anything, just come with us.' Still no response. Martha walked around to the other side of the bed and saw her friend staring off into nothing, breathing but otherwise showing no sign of life whatsoever. 'I know you can hear me. You better get your arse up and out of that bed. We are not leaving you behind no matter how pathetic you think you have become. One day soon you'll realise you're being a complete and utter idiot and then you can apologise, but for now, get up and get out of that door.' Martha ended up shouting which of course upset the two little ones in her arms, but it also made Ruth's eyes widen in surprise as she got up and woodenly walked out of the door.

'Alright, dear?' Jean asked.

'Let's go,' Martha replied tightly, trying to soothe the children she was carrying whilst bristling in anger that

Ruth was allowed to give up like that. Not on her watch.

There were two skimmers waiting for them, down at pavement level. It took two trips to bring down all the luggage and equipment. They left the NanNan behind. Martha felt that Kira and Jed wouldn't look too favourably upon the robot being used in Camp Eden and she hoped that all the childcare wouldn't fall firmly on her shoulders. Just because she was no longer governor did not mean she had a burning desire to become governess to four children. Malcolm got in with the luggage while the women and children took the second skimmer. They were both armoured, both had tinted windows, and both had armed guards. Clearly Jed's team were taking no risks. Not that Martha was expecting any trouble. No-one, apart from Ben and Chief Minkov, knew they were leaving the city and she was certain the chief was loyal to the citizens of 42 and had no connections or ties to Corporation whatsoever. He was a good man and reminded her of her late father. She wished she could have spent longer getting to know him or at least had the chance to say goodbye properly.

The skimmers finally left the building and began their journey out of the city. They attracted little attention and without the force-field in place were able to leave freely and travel onwards to Camp Eden. No-one in the skimmers noticed the lone spy drone watching and recording them leaving.

MSCHILD: Why is Hamble leaving the city? So what if GJENK said she could have the child. Are there no laws?

ANON17: Let them go. We don't need them. 42 is better off without them.

NEWCORP: Thank you for welcoming New Corporation. City 15 has ceased to operate. New Corporation looks forward to making City 42 great again.

C42N: This sweep channel has been deactivated.

ANON40: What happened to City 15?

CORPSECURITY: We will now replace FORCE for all your safety & security needs. Same location, new team. We will protect & serve City 42.

FORCE: This sweep channel has been deactivated.

ANON40: Seriously - what happened to City 15?

ANON40: This sweep channel has been deactivated.

SMAC: The sweeps are experiencing a few technical difficulties. Nothing to worry about.

ENCRYPTED MESSAGE FROM 7421 TO NEW CORP
>>*They've left the city. Hamble and Maddocks, the children and some ex-Force Operatives loyal to Jenkins. Do you want me to pursue?*<<

ENCRYPTED MESSAGE FROM NEW CORP TO 7421
>>I AM AWARE OF YOUR INCOMPETENCE. WHY DID YOU NOT REACTIVATE THE FORCEFIELD?<<

ENCRYPTED MESSAGE FROM 7421 TO NEW CORP
>>*It was the next item on the list - I'm sorry, I've been dealing with the sweep accounts. And anyway, where would they go? You can track them, can't you? Bring them back.*<<

ENCRYPTED MESSAGE FROM NEW CORP TO 7421
>>WE ARE WATCHING EVERYTHING. I WILL DEAL WITH THE NON-CONFORMERS IN DUE COURSE. REMOVE MINKOV FROM OFFICE. BEGIN ROLLING OUT THE NEURAL IMPLANTS<<

ENCRYPTED MESSAGE FROM 7421 TO NEW CORP
>>*Already? The infrastructure isn't in place for the implants. Corp Tech has still not been properly reformed - maybe we should wait a while, get the medical supply situation under control?*<<

ENCRYPTED MESSAGE FROM NEW CORP TO

141

7421
\>\>YOU HAVE YOUR ORDERS. EVERYTHING ELSE WILL BE DEALT WITH\<\<

Chapter 18

'Ma! You made it. Have you come to see us off?' Dina was delighted to see Martha at Camp Eden.

'No. I'm here to join you,' replied Martha as she watched Kira run to hug her parents.

'Join us? That's amazing! Which city do you want to go to?'

Martha shrugged. She'd been so focused on getting to Camp Eden, she hadn't thought about the new mission to reach out to other cities. After Ben had warned her about using the comms link, she hadn't checked in with Jed, but they could work out the detailed plan of action now everyone was here. She looked down at the little boy in her arms and knew she needed to go and find Jed before she did anything else. Smiling at Dina she wandered further into the camp.

Jed stood with Ash, looking at some maps on the camp's vid screen. The two men were completely absorbed in what they were doing and didn't hear Martha approach. She coughed quietly.

Ash turned and grinned at Martha, made his excuses and left them to it. Jed tutted at Ash breaking his concentration then realised who else was there.

'Is that... Is that him?' His voice sounded hoarse.

'Jed, meet Peter, your nephew.' Martha held out the little boy to his uncle. The child responded by stretching out his little arms and gurgling happily.

Tears pricked Jed's eyes as he took the boy and began talking to him softly. Martha watched for a few moments then quietly left them alone. They needed time to bond and get to know each other.

Dina grabbed her elbow and spun her round.

'Come on, we're all in the communal tent. Moham's making tea.' Dina chattered happily as she led Martha over to where the others had gathered. Jean and Malcolm had bought Lucas and Sarah to the tent and were making a huge fuss over Grace who they hadn't seen for at least three days. Ruth was sitting listlessly to one side. Kira was nowhere to be seen. Dina saw Martha looking around.

'Kira's gone to meet Peter. That's such a great name by the way. Is he a good baby?' Dina asked.

'He's been an angel, so far at least. Considering how much change has happened to him,' replied Martha.

Moham pressed hot tea into Ruth's hands and she looked up at him curiously. Then she seemed to remember who he was and where she was. She took a sip of tea and began to look around, taking in her surroundings. Dina made to go and speak to her, but Martha held her back.

'Not yet, let her have her tea. Come and see the kids with me.'

Dina didn't need much encouragement to go and play. Soon excited gurgles were echoing across the camp.

Kira joined them with young Peter in her arms. 'Isn't he adorable? Don't you think he looks like Pete? With Ingrid's eyes though.'

Martha nodded. 'Where's Jed?'

'He's gone to sort out the operatives. The camp is pretty full now, we don't want to overrun the experiments or destroy any of the natural habitats so Moham is helping him get everything worked out.' Kira watched the children playing together for a moment before continuing. 'He thinks we should talk about next steps when the kids have all gone to bed, what do you think?'

'I think that would be the best idea. Too distracting otherwise,' replied Martha.

The women spent the next few hours happily playing with the children, getting dinner organised and then putting their precious families into bed. They had just sat down to talk about what they were going to do next when one of Jed's operatives came running up.

'Sir? We've got a drone at the edge of camp.'

Jed leapt up. 'A drone? Show me.'

The others followed to see what the commotion was. There hovering on the edge of camp was a spy drone.

'How long has it been there?' asked Jed.

'Hard to tell, Sir. We noticed it about five minutes ago and I came straight to find you and report it.'

Jed frowned. It didn't look like one of theirs, it was more compact and if anything, looked more expensive. Martha pushed through the others and came to stand next to Jed.

'What do you think?' she asked.

But before he had chance to answer a tinny voice issued from the drone.

'Ms Hamble. So good to see you. I had hoped to make your acquaintance in City 42 but alas by the time I arrived, you had already left. I see you have surrounded yourself with an illegal militia, some women and several children. A rather odd selection, don't you think?'

'And who exactly am I talking to?' Martha asked.

'Well now, that's privileged information. If you'd stayed in the city, maybe we could've built a wonderful friendship. Alas, now I must treat you as an enemy of New Corporation.'

Dina and Kira looked at each frowning. Dina mouthed the question 'New Corporation?' but Kira shrugged. She didn't know what it meant either.

'Why am I your enemy?' asked Martha.

'You were instrumental in an illegal takeover, were you not? You put yourself in charge, did you not? I believe all four members of the Board delegated to look after City 42 perished, have they not? Your father amongst them. I am surprised. I never thought a lady such as yourself would have patricide listed amongst her crimes.'

Martha reddened but chose not to answer. She knew she hadn't killed her father. The others came to stand closer to her, trying to offer moral support without saying anything.

'What do you want?' asked Jed.

'Ah, the newly appointed Captain of the Guard. You do realise that your new position is bogus and all the operatives you have with you have been officially listed as deserters.'

'Corporation have no jurisdiction over Force,' replied Jed.

'Times change. We do now. I'm afraid your Chief has stepped down from office. Ill health apparently. He doesn't have long left.'

Kira put a warning hand on Jed's arm, and he swallowed his retort. The drone continued.

'I am here to inform you that you have two choices.

You either leave Camp Eden within the next twenty-four hours and try your luck out there in the wilderness or you return to City 42 where you will be tried for your crimes against New Corporation. Make the right decision and we may show mercy. I warn you though, if you attempt to make contact with another New Corporation city you will be arrested. New Corporation does not tolerate activists.'

'Is that why you destroyed City 15?' shouted Dina, overcome with emotion.

Ruth turned pale as she wavered on her feet while Martha cursed inwardly. That was not how she had planned to tell Ruth about what had happened.

'City 15 were warned multiple times. But your fearless leader sealed their fate and accelerated their decimation by attempting to reach out and make contact. We will not tolerate any alternatives to New Corporation rule.'

There was silence. The group had a lot of questions, but no-one felt like talking to the drone any further.

'I see you are taking a moment. Let me help with that. I remind you that you have twenty-four hours to return to City 42 where the children will be confiscated, and you will all be held for questioning. If we are satisfied that you are no longer a threat to New Corporation you will be security tagged, separated and assigned new roles within the city. Your children may or may not be assigned back to you.'

Ruth surprised everyone by interrupting the drone. 'You can't do that! You can't take away my child. She's biologically mine, I grew her - no thanks to your experimentations.'

'Be that as it may, Ms Maddocks. Your recent overdose brings into question your fitness as a parent.'

147

There was a long silence. The drone remained hovering in place, watching each and every one of them.

'Twenty-four hours,' the tinny voice announced before the drone flew abruptly away.

Stunned, Jed looked for his wife and pulled her into an embrace. Dina was clinging to Max and Ruth had gone to stand with Martha who had a determined look on her face.

'It's time to break camp,' she announced but Ruth blocked her path.

'It's time for you to tell me what happened in City 15,' she said. The others gave the two women a wide berth as Martha quietly explained what had happened to all the people in City 15. Ruth shook her head at first, unable to comprehend the brutality, then as she realised Martha was telling the truth, she began to cry. It was a sombre reminder to everyone else how ruthless New Corporation were.

'It's horrible, Ruth, I still can't believe it happened. Like it should have been a dream,' Dina said, trying to help comfort her friend with a hug as she walked with Ruth and Martha back over to some chairs. Kira came to join them with some hot, sweet tea so Martha used the opportunity to slip away and find Jed. They met in the communal tent.

'How many men do you have, Jed? How many skimmers?' Martha's voice was all business. Internally she was deeply shaken by the casual show of force New Corporation had demonstrated. This was a different kind of Corporation to what she was used to. Yes, the previous regime had been instrumental in treating the water supply and keeping everyone sterile, but she truly believed that had been a result of circumstance rather than malicious intent. What had happened in City 15

148

didn't feel like the Corporation she had grown up with but, she didn't have time to think about that now. She needed to focus on getting everyone to safety.

'I've got twenty operatives, so I'd split them down the middle. Ten to each mission? I'll head up one team, put Ash in charge of the other,' replied Jed.

'It's a pity we don't have two Ashes - we could do with his tech expertise, especially in maintaining comms between the two teams. If such things are possible,' mused Martha.

'We might not have two Ashes, but Dina is pretty quick on the uptake, she's been watching what Ash has been doing. I reckon he could get her up to speed quickly enough.'

'Okay so... does that mean we split Dina and Max up?'

'You talking about us?' Dina asked in a cheery voice as she joined the conversation, making Martha jump.

'We're trying to organise the two teams,' she said.

'Well, surely you need all of us to chip in, tell you what we think.'

'I'm sorry, Dina. We don't have time for that kind of delegation and discussion. Jed and I are taking charge.'

Dina's face fell. 'Will we at least have a say after you've made the decision for us?'

Martha shook her head. 'It's not up for public debate.' She deliberately turned away from her friend, feeling awful for doing so but knowing that if they waited for everyone to have their say, the twenty-four hours deadline would come and go. Dina stalked away.

'I'd like to stay with Kira,' Jed stated.

'I figured as much. You and Kira can head out to City 36. Take Dina with you.'

'So you are splitting up Dina and Max then? They

won't be happy about that.'

Martha put her head in her hands. She could feel the stress weighing down on her. 'Fine.' She looked up. 'Call everyone together, Jed. I assume your team will at least do as they're told?'

Jed nodded and went to round the others up. It didn't take long; they had been hovering nearby.

'Right, this is the situation,' began Martha. 'As you heard, we have less than twenty-four hours to break camp and get out of here. I don't know whether they will try to destroy us like they did City 15, but I am certainly not going to take that risk.'

'Does this mean you've decided to let us decide for ourselves what we want to do?' Dina asked.

Martha felt stung by Dina's words, but she couldn't blame her. 'We will be splitting up into two missions, one to City 9, the other to City 36. We do not know what to expect from either city. We will be at opposite ends of the country and each team will have to deal with any problems they uncover themselves. So, if you volunteer for a particular city, you need to understand that it's not easy to turn around and go somewhere else instead.'

The group were silent.

'Anyone have a preference?' Martha asked.

'I would like to go to City 36,' Kira stated calmly. 'I'll take Grace, Peter and my parents with me.' She did not mention Jed.

'We want to go to City 9,' Dina announced, grabbing Max's hand and speaking with a slight lift to her chin, expecting some kind of disagreement.

'I think the greater Corporation presence will be at City 9. Are you sure you feel confident enough to face that?' Martha asked.

Dina nodded.

'I think Ruth and Sarah should go with you, Kira.' Martha turned to Ruth for her agreement, but she looked back with emotionless eyes. It didn't make any difference to Ruth where she went.

'What about you?' Kira asked. 'If you think City 9 is going to be a strong base for Corporation, I don't think you should go there. You're a wanted woman now. We all are.'

'Exactly why you're going to take Lucas and I'm going to City 9. And Jed is coming with me.'

No-one said anything. Everyone waited to see Jed's reaction. Kira grabbed his hand tightly and he pulled her into a quick embrace. Then he nodded curtly and took over the rest of the discussion.

'Ash, you're headed up to 36,' Jed said. 'Brief Dina on the comms system. Let's try and get a secure connection established now before we head out.' Then he walked off to split his operatives into two teams and oversee the distribution of supplies and vehicles. The team heading out to 36 would need more than those going to 9. Jed knew Martha was right, but he was still disappointed. He didn't want to be apart from his wife now they'd been threatened by New Corp and he'd only just met Peter. But taking the children to 9 was too much of a risk. A small voice in his head wondered whether they were making a mistake by putting all their children together, but Kira seemed certain that 36 was more likely to be out from under Corporation control. There was no tactical advantage for Corporation to have a strong foothold in a city in the middle of a remote mountain range. The people that lived there were likely to be more self-reliant than those in City 42.

They had to try and find somewhere safe, find someone who could teach them the skills they would need to survive. The fight with Corporation wasn't over but they were woefully underprepared if the causal show of force demonstrated by the faceless drone voice was anything to go by.

'Ruth? Ruth?' Jean called out. There was no response. 'I do not know what to do with that girl, Malcolm.'

Her husband patted her arm in sympathy as the two of them tried to chivvy Ruth along.

'Come along, Ruth. You need to stow your gear in the right skimmer. Make sure Sarah has everything she needs.' Jean peered up at the blank faced woman. 'You do care about your daughter, don't you?' Again, no response. Jean threw her hands up in despair and turned to go, then had second thoughts and took Sarah out of Ruth's arms. 'Come along baby girl, let's get you some milk before we have to leave.'

Ruth made no move to stop her. She was still trying to process the fact that Sarah's father and the dozens of other people she knew from City 15 were all dead. Nothing felt real. Cigarette smoke drifted past her face, making her nose twitch. She blinked in surprise and looked beside her. Malcolm had sparked up and was offering her a drag. Ruth took the cigarette with shaky fingers; it had been months since she'd smoked. She inhaled deeply, savouring the hot smoke.

'You know, that little girl needs you,' said Malcolm. Ruth continued to smoke in silence.

'It's just...' she said finally.

'Yep.'

'And I don't know if I can.' Ruth's voice was quiet as she admitted her own fear of not being able to be there for her daughter.

Malcolm ground the cigarette stub into the floor

with the heel of his shoe.

'None of us know for sure, love. We have to do the best we can.' Malcolm passed over the half full cigarette carton. 'Come on, we've got to find a place to hide those before Jean kills me.'

Ruth gave a small laugh and followed him back to the tents. While she helped Jean and Martha pack up all the baby bits and pieces, Dina was getting a quick but intense tech lesson from Ash.

'It's pretty simple, these comms are designed to work on a different frequency to the ones Corporation use but that doesn't mean they won't switch. You'll be able to tell if they are by the opening tone, listen.' Ash turned on the comms system and it clicked twice. 'Two clicks and we're okay, any more or less and it's not a safe channel.' He dug around in his pockets for an info jack. 'This has a list of subsequent channels to try should the first one get compromised.'

'What if they all get compromised?' asked Dina nervously.

'We won't use the comms too often,' replied Jed, as he came to join them. 'You happy with how everything works, Dina?'

'Yeah, I think so.'

'Good. Go make sure you've both got everything you need. We need to get moving.' Jed watched as the camp bustled before him. They were leaving the main Camp Eden scientists behind, there wasn't room to take everyone with them and Jed was hoping New Corporation would leave them alone. After all, Camp Eden had originally been a Corporation idea. He beckoned to Max to come with him as he walked by.

'Hey, Max. Can you run through the testing kit with Ash please? I want to make sure he knows how to test the air and water as they're travelling and once they get to City 36.'

'Yeah of course. We've got two kits; it makes sense for them to take one.' Max hurried to get the equipment and was soon taking Ash through the basics. It was simple enough, as long as he sampled correctly the machine would do the rest.

With everything packed, the two teams were ready to go. All that remained was to say goodbye. Jean hugged everyone, regardless of whether they were coming with her or not. No-one minded, it was comforting. Dina and Kira hugged, the children were peppered with kisses and had no idea what was going on. Max shook hands with Ash and wished him luck, Jed finished briefing the team headed out to City 36. Ruth was crying, happy and sad tears mingled together as she hugged Martha tight. Everyone was ready to go; it was just Kira and Jed left to say goodbye.

'Are you going to be alright?' Kira asked him.

Jed laughed softly. 'It should be me asking you that.' He paused. 'Have you got everything? For Grace? And the others?'

'Mm, we should be alright. We've got half the dried food and a treatment system for water. All the milk for the kids. Reusable nappies. I'm confident City 36 will be able to re-supply us.'

Jed gathered his wife in his arms and held her close. He smelled her hair and tried to take comfort in the fact that they were doing the right thing. He hoped. He wasn't going to ask what Kira would do if City 36 didn't exist anymore. His wife was resourceful.

Chapter 19

Sean looked out of the window at City 42 with pleasure. They'd finally painted over that awful Gaia graffiti on the wall across from Collection. He was going to be in charge now and he would be putting New Corporation rule firmly in place. There was bound to be the odd objection, but the citizens would accept the new neural implants and anything else New Corp implemented.

'Here's your synth-caf, Sean.'

'Thanks, Jon. Is everything ready for the meeting?'

'Yes. Do you think we'll have to have the implants as well?' asked Jon, Sean's aide.

'I don't think so. New Corp know we're loyal to them, it shouldn't be a problem,' Sean replied but he was slightly anxious about the implants. They were designed to dampen down independent thinking and therefore negate any thoughts about disloyalty to New Corp, keep citizens more docile and less likely to question anything. 'They'll want us able to think independently, Jon. After all, we'll be running the city.'

'Are you're going to say yes then, when they offer you the governorship?'

Sean puffed out his chest a little. 'Of course. Hamble made a mess of things, dismantling the HER water treatment plant - telling women they could have children. Look what happened there. Nothing. Just bitter disappointment.' He turned away from the window with a smile. 'With Corp Medical back in firm control, we'll be able to neutralise any embryos created outside the designated population growth lines. People can't be allowed to just create life wantonly.' He gazed at the meeting table, then frowned. 'Shouldn't there be snacks?'

Jon mumbled an affirmative and hurried out to get some organised. Sean checked his wristplant. The New Corp board members should be arriving soon. He was sure appointment to governor after everything he'd done was a mere formality. Subduing the Chief of Force had been more difficult than expected. Minkov inspired terrific loyalty in his team, but they'd managed to remove him from office. Fortunately for Sean, the chief had been too busy promoting Jenkins and creating his ridiculous mini militia to pay full attention to the influx of Corp loyal operatives and the move to becoming Corp Security. Minkov and his handful of loyal detectives had been unable to stand up to that show of force. Ha Force. What a ridiculous name, thought Sean. That would be the first thing to change. Corp Security worked well enough in City 9 it would work fine here.

The door to the conference room swung open. Three men and a woman walked into the room. The woman was thin, her steel-grey hair cut in a smart bob, her face devoid of any warmth. She looked at Sean then cocked a finger. One of the men on her right took out a scanner and walked towards him. Sean raised his hands in the air in submission and took half a step backwards.

'What's this?' he asked.

'Just checking for bugs,' the man replied.

The woman walked around the board room. She wiped her finger across the table and seemed surprised when it came back clean. The scanner beeped once, and the man pocketed the device. She looked at him and he shook his head. The woman sniffed and sat down at the head of the table, gesturing for Sean to join her.

'My name is Clarity Jones,' she said. 'I am the Chief Executive of the Board of Directors for Corporation owned City 42. Tell me, Mr MacIntyre, why was the rebel governor not apprehended?'

'I, uh, well, I didn't think she would leave the city and I thought...'

'That seems to have been your problem.' Ms Jones steepled her fingers. 'I believe your instructions were clear, to initiate the vote of no confidence and dismantle the fake government. It wasn't to allow everyone to leave the city freely and go who knows where. What exactly gave you difficulty?'

'But you sent the drone, to Camp Eden! You already know where they are.' Sean looked at the men who had entered the room with Ms Jones for support, but they

157

remained standing still, blank faced yet alert.

'We did indeed, Mr MacIntyre. It may, however, be a case of too little, too late,' replied Ms Jones calmly.

'It doesn't matter if they don't come back. If they go out into the wild, they'll just die of radiation poisoning. We can harass them with drones and keep them moving, they'll soon run out of supplies.' Sean tried to sound confident.

'You seem to think the resources of New Corp are expressly available to clear up your mess. New Corp Militia is not your private clean-up crew.'

'No, but, but there are resources and, and...' Sean dropped his head and fell silent. This was not how he had expected this meeting to go. The silence dragged. 'Anyway, there's nowhere for them to go. City 9 is New Corp and if they try to go to City 36, they'll die faster. I don't see why you're so worried.' Sean sounded sulky. 'We can always threaten the family they left behind, make them come back.'

Ms Jones tilted her head to one side. 'Left behind?'

Sean warmed to his idea. 'Yes. We can apprehend whoever it is, threaten them or something and then they'll be forced to come back.'

'I see. And what family members does Martha Hamble have left?'

'Her mother.'

Ms Jones nodded. 'Yes, Mrs Hamble is a staunch supporter of New Corp and has funded many of our projects. I understand relationships between her and her daughter are strained at best.'

'Alright, alright, bad example.' Sean started thinking aloud. 'Dina Grey's family was lost in the City 15 riots and Ruth Maddocks lost her only link in the recent sanitation.' He started pacing. 'What about the Jenkins?'

Ms Jones regarded Sean coolly. 'Gretchen Jenkins is to be sworn in as a new board member today. I doubt we will be able to threaten her or something.'

'Okay, okay. We can't threaten Kira Jenkins parents - they left with her... but, there's a cousin!' He faced Ms Jones in triumph. 'We could use him as leverage.'

Ms Jones gestured imperiously for a handheld from one of her attendants. She swiped the screen a few times then read aloud.

'Ben Jenkins, last remaining Anti-Corp activist, cousin to Jed Jenkins. Linked with disrupting sweeps, infiltration at Force and known to be highly skilled in data stream interfacing.' She raised her head to look at Sean. 'Attempts were made to apprehend Mr Jenkins this morning. He has been terminated.'

'He's what? But...' Sean was momentarily dumbfounded but quickly rallied. 'It doesn't matter. They won't come back here, and I doubt very much they will survive out there. I don't see why we need to be so worried.'

'I am concerned, Mr MacIntyre, because these people have left with an idea burning in their little minds. And ideas are dangerous. They lead to free thinking. Corporation was not built on free thinking.'

Sean scoffed a little. 'You don't seriously think anyone will listen to them? Why don't you wipe them out? They're only a bunch of...' Ms Jones cut him off.

'They are a group of well-respected citizens from City 42 who uncovered the sterilisation plot, managed several natural pregnancies and have made alleged contact with the spirit of this planet. Despite our best efforts to keep this information under wraps, it has spread. And even if they don't have all the facts, people will listen.'

'No.' Sean shook his head emphatically. 'They won't. Not once they mention that blue woman nonsense. People will think they're crazy. There's no such thing as spirits of the Earth.'

Ms Jones narrowed her eyes. 'I can see you are perfectly suited for your role as advisor, Mr MacIntyre. Could you organise some synth-caf for the rest of the board members who will be arriving soon? No need to attend. I'm sure you have some important filing to fulfil.' With that she dismissed him from her thoughts, her focus now on the handheld in front of her. One of her personal security caught Sean's eye and jerked his head towards the doorway.

Sean walked woodenly out of the room. This was not what was supposed to have happened. He should be celebrating after being made governor, not dismissed from the meeting room. A small niggle of doubt began to writhe at the back of his mind. Had he done the right thing? His thoughts churned as he began brewing fresh synth-caf for the meeting. It must be some sort of mistake. Ms Jones would soon see he was an invaluable member of the City 42 team. He needed to prove his worth, that was all.

NEWCORP: *For crimes against New Corporation the following individuals are wanted for questioning:*
Martha Hamble
Lucas Hamble
Jed Jenkins
Kira Jenkins
Grace Jenkins
Peter Jenkins
Jean Bishop
Malcolm Bishop

Ruth Maddocks
Sarah Maddocks
Dina Grey
If you see any of these fugitives, your duty to City 42 &
New Corporation requires you to report their
whereabouts immediately. In addition, there are several
people of interest that New Corporation would like to
talk to. Download the list, come forward if mentioned.
Help to keep your city safe.

Chapter 20

It's not safe. It's not safe. It's not safe. Martha woke up in a cold sweat, the warning ringing in her ears. She tried to remember the dream, but it was fading fast. All she was left with was a vague memory of a blue lady. Gaia had spoken to her, warned her. It's not safe. But what wasn't safe?

Dina began tossing and turning, mumbling in her sleep before sitting up abruptly, wide awake. 'It's not safe!' she shouted.

'Did you see her too?' Martha asked.

Dina nodded and took a shaky breath. 'What did Gaia mean? What isn't safe?'

'I don't know but there was something about that dream. It frightened me, Dina.'

'Me too.' The two women hugged, trying to calm themselves down.

'Are we doing the right thing?' asked Martha.

'We are. We'll be at City 9 tomorrow. We've got to get information so we can decide what to do next. You made the best decision, Ma.'

'Did I? What if they decide to kill all the citizens of another city so they can get to us?'

'They won't,' said Jed. He'd woken up and turned his

seat round in the skimmer so he could face them. 'From what we know City 9 is a pro-Corp city. They'll probably know we're there the minute we set foot in the city, but I don't think they'll target us.'

'Won't they arrest us?' asked Dina.

'They could've done that at Camp Eden. They let us go, they must have known we'd head here. I think they're waiting to see what we'll do next,' replied Jed. 'If we keep a low profile and try to blend in as much as possible, I think they'll leave us alone.'

'That doesn't make any sense,' Martha said.

'Yes, it does. Listen. You and Ruth are the first natural parents our city had in decades. Who knows if any of the other cities have had natural pregnancy? You bring hope to so many families wanting children. Plus, Gaia spoke to you. It could be that Corporation are hoping Gaia will show herself again so they can capture her or something.'

Dina scoffed at the idea, but Martha thought Jed might have a point. They spent the rest of the journey in silence. The landscape outside the skimmer window had been flat and featureless except for frequent dead zones of burnt earth. Vegetation had tried to gain purchase here and there, but it was scattered at best. The odd flock of birds swooped through the sky now and then, but they didn't see any larger animals. They hadn't stopped the entire trip, everyone taking turns to navigate and the whole group eating on the move. They'd all felt the urgency to get to City 9 as soon as possible, find out what they could and make a plan for their future.

Leaving the skimmers and all the operatives well outside the city limits; Jed, Max, Dina and Martha entered City 9 on foot. The city force-fields were turned on, but a single gateway allowed visitors through. The

163

security guards didn't seem that interested in their small group. A skimmer had arrived at the same time as them, drawing attention away from the foot traffic so everyone walked through the gateway unobserved, before anyone had chance to change their mind. The city was different to 42 in so many ways, there were no trees or social areas for people to congregate but there were lots of people walking purposefully.

'What do they have on their heads?' asked Max.

'Those are the new neural implants. Ben told me about them,' replied Dina.

Everyone they saw was wearing the new tech which made Martha, Jed and the rest of them stand out for not having them.

'We'll have to get some and mod them. You can do that, can't you, Dina?' asked Jed.

She nodded as they walked further into the city, looking for a nearby shared space. They found an automated building with a free room, so they took it and dumped all their bags, keen to get out and start their mission. Their first step was to upgrade their tech. After leaving the room, they found themselves standing on the edge of a busy plaza.

'New in town?' asked an oily voice. A small man in a scruffy looking grey jumpsuit was standing to one side, his eyes darting left and right as he spoke to them. He looked like the kind of person they needed to avoid but also the type of person who would be able to help them out.

Martha shrank back and let Jed do the talking.

'We need to upgrade - think you can point us in the right direction?'

'Name's Marv and tech upgrades are my speciality. This way.' The shifty man gestured for the group to follow him. He led them off the main street through a side passage which skirted but did not go down any of the tight looking alleys. Martha began to think they might actually get what they needed.

After a few minutes they stopped outside a small shop. A faded auto-ad was flickering in the window, made even harder to see by the layer of grime over both window and door. The man held the door open and everyone filed in. Jed was pleased he'd left the rest of the team outside the city limits with the skimmers. They needed to maintain a low profile here.

The shop looked like nothing special from the outside but inside it was a tech lover's dream. It had everything - the latest wristplant, integrated arm swipes, retina sweeps as well as the one thing they didn't have any of. They latest tech from New Corp. Neural implants.

'So whaddaya need?' The man sensed he was going to make a small fortune and he wasn't wrong. By the time Jed had bought some neural implants and new wristplants for himself, Martha, Dina and Max, the seller's grin was as wide as his face.

'Do you need help fitting them?' The man peered at the side of Jed's head. 'Looks like you've not had one before.'

'Er, no, thank you. We can manage.' Jed handed over the requested tokens and the small group tried to remember how to get back to the lodgings they'd checked into near the entrance to the town. No-one was about as they accessed their shared room. They hadn't felt comfortable splitting up even though it was a tight squeeze, all of them together. Now that they'd made it to City 9, they didn't want to take any risks. Gaia's warning still resonated with Dina and Martha and the men had

165

seen how shaken up they'd been. Everyone knew they needed to be careful in this city.

'Do you think you can deactivate these, Dina?' Jed asked, pointing to the neural implants on the table.

'I think so. If the information Ben sent is correct and these are the same model, it should be straightforward enough. I need a little space.' She shooed everyone away from the small table and set to work. In Ben's last communique he'd explained how New Corp was rolling out the neural implants to every citizen and had outlined the basics of deactivating them. No-one had heard from Ben in a couple of days and Jed had been reluctant to send any unnecessary messages. There was a good chance New Corp knew where they were, so there was no need to be blatant and advertise the fact. And with New Corp cracking down on non-conformers there was no way they could walk around City 9 without the neural implants in evidence. They'd be noticed. It was bad enough their clothing wasn't the same as what everyone else was wearing, but at least they could stick to their story of being travellers. City 9 must have travellers being so close to the coast. Martha still held on to the hope they would find transport away from this island. It would mean waiting for Kira and the rest to finish up in 36 and travel back down the length of the country but it was a small price to pay for escaping Corporation rule. She was excited about going out tomorrow to explore and see what they could find out.

The loudspeaker announcement made them all jump. 'Curfew in ten minutes. Curfew in ten minutes. All outer doors will be locked. All outer doors will be locked.'

'Well, that was unexpected,' Jed commented. 'I'm going to have a shower.' And he locked himself into the bathroom. Dina had her head bent over the components of the neural implants, leaving Martha and Max with nothing to do.

'Shall we see what's on the news sweeps or did you want to order some food?' Max asked.

'Let's find something to eat. There's bound to be something that everyone will like,' replied Martha.

The two of them checked the small screen nestled on the wall next to the synth-caf machine. The options were all the same sorts of instant, dried food variety they used to eat in 42. Martha felt a stab of disappointment. She had thought that with City 9 being by the coast, there might have been some hint of fresh fish available to eat. But then she considered their team hadn't had chance to check out the local area thoroughly. The one thing they had been able to clear was the water supply. It was contaminant free, thank goodness.

Every time a drone passed the window of their room, Martha flinched. She couldn't help it. She knew New Corp would probably have tabs on all of them but if their luck held New Corp might leave them alone while they were here. They couldn't return to 42, where they would stand trial for their crimes. But she didn't know what New Corp would do now they'd travelled to City 9.

Martha let Max order the food. It all tasted the same to her anyway. She made sure the synth-caf machine was fully stocked. She didn't think they'd get much sleep tonight and she wanted to make sure she was as caffeinated as possible.

Two hours later and Dina uttered an exalted 'Yes!' bringing everyone over to her small table.

'I've done it! They won't try to change the neural pathways anymore, but they'll still look like everyone else's. Max, come here.' She beckoned him to come closer and as he bent down towards her, she moved his

167

hair out of the way and fixed the implant in place. 'It has self-adhesive nanos which are separate to the ones that change the neural pathways. These ones don't think for themselves, they just stick,' she explained. 'Give it a shake!'

Max shook his head a little then, feeling braver moved his head around rapidly. The implant stayed in place. 'Well done, D.' He smiled at her.

Dina grinned back at him. 'Come on you two, let's get these fitted then someone can put mine on.' Martha stepped forward first while Jed grabbed some more food from the replicator so they could eat and discuss their next step.

'At least we look a bit more like everyone else now,' he commented once his implant was in place. 'Are we all clear on the plan for tomorrow?'

'Yes, Max is going to try and reach the ocean, we need to see whether it's cordoned off or whether citizens have free access. We also need to find out what condition the water is in,' Martha said.

'Fine with me,' replied Max. 'If I run into any problems, I'll flash my scientist card at them. It usually confuses low level enforcers enough to leave me alone.'

'But you've got your panic button just in case?' asked Jed.

Max nodded. They had all had them installed on the way to City 9, deep in the left armpit so they couldn't be set off by accident.

'Me and Ma are going to see if we can find any fresh food,' said Dina.

'Plus, two women shopping for food will be less conspicuous then if we send Jed,' teased Martha.

There was a brief chuckle from Jed. 'I'm going to try and do a loop of the city. See how big it is, what other

168

exits and entrances there are, whether there are any obvious weak spots. It will be good to see whether there is Force here or if it's New Corp Security. We need to resupply in case of a quick getaway. Our food sachets are running low.' Everyone nodded in agreement, happy with their assignments.

'I still can't wrap my head around New Corp,' Dina said. 'I mean, I understand they felt they had to retaliate against the uprising in 42. That makes sense to me. But why rebrand?'

'If they rebranded at all.' Martha chipped in. 'They could be another arm of a massive worldwide conglomerate. Or they could be a takeover company, trying to keep things feeling similar so there is less panic. New Corp feel very different to me.' She paused, checking she had everyone's attention. 'We can't forget 15.'

Dina shook her head and reached out for Max's hand to squeeze in comfort. They would never forget City 15.

ENCRYPTED MESSAGE FROM CITY 9 TO CITY 42
>>*Martha Hamble, Dina Grey & Jed Jenkins have entered City 9*<<

ENCRYPTED MESSAGE FROM CITY 42 TO CITY 9
>>FOLLOW THEM AND REPORT BACK<<

ENCRYPTED MESSAGE FROM CITY 9 TO CITY 42
>>*Do you want us to apprehend them for questioning?*<<

ENCRYPTED MESSAGE FROM CITY 42 TO CITY 9
>>NOT YET. LET'S SEE WHAT THEY DO. THEY MIGHT LEAD US TO THE RESISTANCE<<

Chapter 21

Kira smiled. She was suspended in a warm, dark place, gently floating but it didn't feel scary. She felt safe and content. The darkness became lighter as a soft golden glow expanded from everywhere at once. Colours flooded her awareness and Kira realised she was now floating above the Earth, holding hands with her blue lady. She was with Gaia. And she was dreaming.

'We've missed you so much. Why haven't you shown yourself? Guided us? We need you!' exclaimed Kira.

The blue lady smiled sadly, and a tear rolled down her face. She turned to look the other way and Kira saw a deep cut down the side of Gaia's neck, over her shoulder and disappearing down her back. It was black and dull with grey shadows pulsing either side of the gash. Kira put a hand out to help but then faltered.

'You're too weak. You haven't healed enough yet. Can we help in some way?' she asked.

Gaia turned to look at her again and her entire face was transformed by a glowing smile as she nodded. Kira felt excited.

'We're trying to find a new place to live, somewhere free of Corporation where we can raise the children and... and... I don't know, help you heal somehow.'

Gaia put out a hand and touched Kira's face gently before she started to fade, still smiling.

Kira woke slowly, basking in the remnants of her dream, feeling her spirit refreshed.

'You look happy,' commented Ruth. 'Dreaming of Jed?'

'No. It was Gaia, she came to me - oh, Ruth! She hasn't forgotten us. She needs our help to heal herself and us finding somewhere to live is all part of it, I just know it.' Kira's face glowed in excitement, but Ruth was less enthusiastic, and half nodded.

'Well, we're here,' she said.

Kira scrambled out of the skimmer in excitement. But City 36 wasn't so much a city as a collection of huts and by the looks of things, they had all been abandoned some time ago. Kira was so disappointed. She had pinned her hopes on finding a group of people out here, who had learned to be self-sufficient and live off the land with no involvement whatsoever from Corporation. Maybe even be without technology. Instead, all she had were derelict huts that looked like they wouldn't survive the next five minutes let alone a harsh winter. There were even abandoned beehives.

Ash came to join her; he'd finished making his sweeps.

'There's nothing here. I'm sorry Kira. There's no sign of there ever being a force-field or a comms network or any kind of technology that we would recognise. It's also a dead zone for our comms. Are you sure this is the right place?'

'According to the Archives it is.' She surveyed the ruins in dismay. 'Do we have enough supplies to make it back to the others? They will be in City 9 by now. It seems we split up for no reason.'

'We should have, but... something feels odd about this place, don't you think?' Ash shivered. 'I mean think about it. Why have the city listed in the archives if there is absolutely nothing here? And I'm not being funny but these huts, as much as they look like they're about to fall down in disrepair, they also look like they've only just been put together. Out of old wood but... there's something here that's not right.'

'You're very observant, friend.' A new voice startled Kira and Ash who turned to stare a gun barrel in the face. Behind the gun was a gruff looking man, wrapped up against the chill, his moustache bristling as he gestured with the rifle. 'How many of you are there?'

'Why? Who are you?' demanded Ash.

'Name's Tomas.' The man narrowed his eyes. 'I'll ask you again, how many are with you?'

'Fourteen adults. Four children.' Kira held her hands out in supplication, hoping that the mention of children would generate enough sympathy to at least allow them to leave.

'Children?' Tomas seemed surprised. He lowered his weapon. 'You'd better come with me.' He turned and walked away without waiting to see if they were following him. Kira and Ash stared at each other. Should they follow? At the rise of the hill, Tomas turned back and gestured impatiently. Kira shrugged. She'd come all this way to find a new kind of civilisation. It appeared it had found her. She went to the communal skimmer to get Grace and tell the others. She decided they could carry the children, rather than use the strollers, not knowing what the terrain would be like. It meant Ash had to carry Peter, but he didn't seem to mind. In fact, all of the operatives were rather taken with the little fella.

The operatives piled out of their skimmer, wearing

minimal gear. It looked unthreatening but in reality, they were well armed to protect the rest of the group.

Tomas had not waited for them at the top of the hill and had begun his descent. The group quickly followed him.

'Are you sure this is a good idea, love? We could be walking into who knows what, do you even know that man's name? And is that a gun he's holding? I'm not sure about this at all, Kira. Think of the children. We can't run headlong into things. You're meant to be being responsible.' Jean was concerned.

'His name is Tomas, Mum, and I know, but we've come all this way. I refuse to believe there is no settlement of any kind here. These people could be our future,' replied Kira.

'Or they could be our end. I think we should leave some of us behind. As a security measure.' Ruth joined the conversation, which surprised everyone.

'We'll be fine. Ruth, remember that vision I told you about? From Gaia? I think this is what she meant. I have to take the first step here. It will be worth it; I can feel it.'

Neither Kira's mum nor Ruth looked convinced. Jean fell back to keep an eye on Ruth who was still withdrawn although she had begun to take a little interest in caring for Sarah and was carrying her at the moment.

Kira dragged her attention back to the direction the strange man had gone and realised he'd disappeared. She faltered and stopped descending. The operatives had fanned out ahead and Ash was staying back with Kira and the others. One of the operatives gave a shout and beckoned the others over. There was a cave opening set into the hill. Tomas reappeared at the mouth of the cave.

'Well, come if you're coming,' he said. And stomped

off back the way he had come.

Ash split the operatives up, some in front, some flanking and some in the rear. They were all well trained and knew they had precious cargo to protect as they entered the cave.

It was like nothing Kira had been expecting. The cave felt warm and dry with light brackets spaced out equally along the wall. As they went further in, Kira became aware of a noise, it sounded like people talking. The tunnel opened out into a large cavern, remodelled into a communal area. There were stalls with goods for sale and some long tables where a handful of people were sitting and chatting. Without realising it, they'd all stopped walking. Everyone gaped at the small, underground community.

'Welcome to Hope.' Tomas was smiling, it made him look a lot less formidable. He'd slung the rifle on his shoulder and was standing in front of the marketplace.

'This isn't City 36?' Kira didn't know whether to be impressed or disappointed.

'City 36 hasn't existed for a long time. We don't answer to the Coalition.'

'Coalition?' whispered Jean to Ruth. 'Who are they?

'They were before Corporation - way before,' Ruth whispered back, her background as a history teacher coming to the rescue.

'Come, let me take you to the elders hall. We'll get you some refreshments and you can meet the rest of the council. Then you can tell us where you've come from and why you're here. Come, please.' Tomas was gesturing for them to follow him again. This time he led them to the left and down a passageway to another, smaller cavern where groups of tables and chairs were arranged in both large and small configurations. There were a few groups of people dotted about but more interesting than that were the two tables on the right-hand side, spread with some food and hot drinks.

'Please, help yourself,' he said, and the group moved towards them eagerly, exclaiming in surprise at the sorts of things available. There were dried fruits and nuts, some hard bread and a large tureen of steaming hot chocolate.

'We ought to check the food first before we eat anything, Kira,' warned Ash.

'Okay, how long will that take?'

'It'll be a couple of hours before the results come back - it's harder to detect anomalies in foodstuffs with the small handhelds,' replied Ash.

'Oh, Ash! I'm sure it will be alright. It doesn't look like there's anything wrong with the food and it would be rude not to.' Carried away in her excitement, Kira left Ash to his doubts and went to join her mum and Ruth in trying some of the fare available.

Ash did not eat anything. He ran his tests.

'This is amazing,' Kira said sipping a cup of hot chocolate as she addressed Tomas. 'Where did all this come from? Did you grow it? Make it?'

'Of course we did. Where else would it have come from?' he asked, a slight frown creasing his brow.

'A food replicator?' replied Kira.

'What's a food replicator?'

'Fascinating,' said Kira. 'Where do you grow your food?' Kira was buzzing, she felt like they'd found what they were looking for and she couldn't wait to tell Jed and the others. This was the place; she could feel it.

'Come, sit, eat. We will introduce ourselves to each other and then we can take you on a tour,' said Tomas, avoiding Kira's question.

The group sat down at one of the larger tables. Tomas smiled and nodded, deflecting their questions with ease. Clearly, he was waiting for more senior members of his settlement to arrive. They didn't wait long.

A dark-haired, slim woman in her fifties hurried into the cavern, she slowed as she caught sight of them and approached, patting her hair and smoothing her dress over her legs. Her gaze lingered on the children before finally turning to address Kira who sat closest to Tomas.

'Welcome to Hope. I don't know how you found us but you are welcome here. You and your children. Tell me, who is in command out there? Is it still Coalition?' The lady sat down in a nearby empty chair.

'Um, I don't...' Kira began to speak but Ruth interrupted so she could explain.

'Coalition were the original governing group that formed after The Event. It was made up of what was left of the various countries' government and military across the globe, who came together in a massive effort to build the cities and leave a legacy.' The woman nodded in agreement, so Ruth continued. 'There has been a lot of speculation as to what exactly had happened to them and how Corporation came to be the overriding power, but the Archives are sketchy at best as to what caused the change in power.' She turned to the woman. 'Basically, Coalition don't exist anymore.'

The women paled and then rallied quickly. 'Where are my manners? Please, I am Gloria, one of the council members here at Hope. I see you've already met Tomas. Do you need more time to recover and rest? I have so many questions.'

'No please, ask away. We have questions of our own. Shall we take turns?' Kira was half joking, but she hoped this woman, this Gloria, would take her seriously.

'Sounds wonderful,' Gloria smiled at her.

Both women spoke at the same time, 'So...' then laughed and Gloria gestured to Kira, 'Please, your turn.'

'How long have you been here?' Kira asked.

'Hope was established soon after the fall of the City 36, the city Coalition had created. Their design wasn't the right fit for this part of the country. Don't get me wrong, Coalition worked hard trying to find a solution for everyone but that was part of the problem. You can't put a one size fits all plaster on the type of problem the world faced. There would be communities that didn't fit within that defined social setting. Plus, the HER radiation was highly toxic this far north. There had been a processing plant up here, used for generating new weapons. It was blown up towards the end of the conflict and decimated the land and waters for miles and miles around.'

Kira was absorbed. 'Didn't you have protection from the radiation?'

'From what we've been able to learn, infrastructure was difficult in the early days. We have often wondered why Coalition wanted to bother with an outpost here, so remote from everyone else and so isolated. You can probably tell that we don't have much tech here. Some old communicators but otherwise, we are self-sufficient. My turn. Where are you from?' Gloria turned her attention on the rest of the group.

'We have travelled from City 42, down in the South. The city was under Corporation control, they are the company who came after Coalition,' replied Kira.

'So, Coalition doesn't exist anymore?'

'No, but I wouldn't get too excited,' replied Kira. 'What followed has not been exactly fair to the remaining populace, at least not in our experience.'

Kira went on to explain how City 42 had been run with the deliberate sterility, the baby lottery and the total control of Corporation over every aspect of everybody's life. The others in her party were content to let her speak. Tomas and Gloria drank in every word. When Kira got to the part about Martha, Ruth and Ingrid's natural births, Gloria clapped her hands together. Kira trailed off, made uncertain by her host's reaction.

'Forgive me,' said Gloria. 'Reproduction has always been a difficult aspect to our community. Obviously, we do procreate, yet radiation levels affected everyone so badly. We've suffered with mutations, genetic deformities and other related medical conditions.'

'How have you managed to overcome them?' asked Ash.

'Everyone is required to have at least four offspring and the gene lines are mixed as much as possible. Obviously, we don't have the scientific equipment to check that our DNA pool is as varied as it could be, but we've done our best. Those matches that resulted in high numbers of defects were soon dissolved. It may sound barbaric, but the survival of our colony has always been at the forefront of everything we've tried to achieve here.'

The visitors took a moment to digest this.

'Why have you come here?' Gloria asked, breaking the silence.

'Martha Hamble, the new governor of City 42, was ousted and it appears Corporation have re-entered our city, as New Corporation this time. But they are more ruthless than before. I don't know if it's the same company as before, it feels like they might have evolved again,' Kira explained. 'There's a lot we don't know.

179

Basically, we were threatened with imprisonment and the reassignment of our children if we stayed. We couldn't stay. It was out of the question. Our group split up to see if we could find any communities out here that had also escaped the total control of Corporation.'

'Where did the others go?'

'They went to the coast, to City 9,' replied Kira.

'I think it's highly unlikely that you will ever see them again.'

'I'm sorry?' Ash asked the question, but everyone was concerned.

'The southern coastal city has always been a stronghold for Coalition. It was the only way to interact with the wider world out there. A real place of power and influence. It doesn't matter what they're calling themselves now, I can guarantee that City 9 will not be a safe place for your friends.' Gloria looked at the children who were happily playing on the floor under the watchful eyes of Jean and Malcolm. 'They don't also have children with them, do they?'

Kira shook her head.

'Come, I can see that all these questions are tiring. Would you like to have a look around?' asked Gloria. 'We have some guest quarters which should be ready for you now as well. I can show you our little community and then leave you to settle in. I'm sure you have lots to process.'

'Thank you, that would be very kind.' A sudden thought occurred to Kira. 'What about our vehicles? We left them by the ruins of 36. Will they be safe there?'

'Tomas will help your men move them. We have several axillary caves for large items such as sledges, carts, that sort of thing. I'm sure your vehicles will fit there. They might attract a lot of interested questions though.' Gloria laughed.

Kira smiled in response but found she couldn't relax fully. It was probably the strangeness of everything and the utter and total lack of a Corporation presence that had her on edge.

'Let's have this tour then.' She smiled brightly at Gloria and stood.

Gloria spoke to Tomas, asking him to find space for their vehicles while Ash organised a couple of operatives to go back with the man to the entrance and help secure the skimmers. The rest of the group gathered themselves together and prepared to be led through Hope. By now, the children were relatively sleepy and snuggled themselves comfortably into their individual carriers. Kira wished she too could be picked up and smooshed but she knew it was important that she paid attention to her surroundings. She activated her cam and smiled at Ash as she noticed him doing the same. They should have some footage to share with the others, at some point, when comms connections were re-established.

'Lead on,' Kira said to Gloria and soon the group crocodiled out of the cavern, most of them eager to see what awaited them elsewhere in this underground grotto but as they exited the cavern, Ash grabbed Kira's arm.

Chapter 22

'I don't think we should follow this Gloria woman further into the cave. We haven't had all of the analysis back yet. I don't think you should've eaten that food. I'm not comfortable with this, Kira. For all we know, we could be walking into danger.'

'But, Ash, don't you feel it? This place is where we're meant to be, I know it.'

Kira was trying to convince herself as well as Ash. This felt like it could be the right place for them, but something was niggling at her.

'I really think we should return to the skimmers. Wait for the results.' Ash sounded so determined to go back that Kira decided to concede.

'Uh, Gloria?' asked Kira. 'Look, the offer of a tour is wonderful, but we need to check in with the other team, make sure our vehicles are secure and get the children ready for bed - I'm sure you understand?'

Gloria faltered and looked back at Kira in disbelief. 'You mean, you don't want to do the rest of the tour?'

'Can't we do it tomorrow?' pleaded Kira.

Gloria patted her hair, obviously reluctant to let them go back to their vehicles. 'Well, I'm sure it will be fine. There's nowhere else for you to go, is there?' And she laughed lightly.

All that did was increase the niggle in Kira's stomach and she suddenly felt relieved that she'd listen to Ash.

'What about first thing in the morning?' suggested Gloria. 'We'll come and collect you for breakfast. It'll be lovely, you can meet our children. They're usually at their best first thing in the morning.' Gloria smiled encouragingly.

Kira nodded while her thoughts whirled. At their best? What did that mean? It did answer one question for her - there were children in Hope.

They turned to go back the way they had come when Kira realised she had no idea what direction she needed to travel in.

'Where is our team please, Gloria?'

'Oh, Greg will show you the way.' Gloria gave a limp wave in their direction at a young man who stood nearby before she turned and left them in the cavern, her shoulders bowed slightly in disappointment.

Kira felt terrible. Was she squandering the opportunity to be part of Gaia's vision for them all? But she had to listen to her team, and she had to listen to her gut. Family came first.

'Ash, do you...' Kira started to speak but Ash motioned her into silence with a curt shake of his head. He hoped she'd get the message. They needed to wait until they got back to the skimmers and could talk in privacy. And get the results of the tests.

They mutely followed Greg through a different set of tunnels to the one they had arrived until he brought them out into a large entrance way. Kira felt relieved to see not only their skimmers but the rest of their team, all together in one place.

Tomas came over to meet them. He pointed to an old-fashioned phone on the wall of the cavern. 'If there's anything you need, just holler on this. One of us will come sort you out.'

'Does this actually work?' Kira asked in wonder.

'Not in the original sense but there'll be someone on the other end who will answer the call, should you need anything.' Tomas waited to see whether they would ask for anything now and when they didn't, he half shrugged and said goodnight, taking Greg with him.

Ash spent a few moments chatting with the operatives who had been sent to get the skimmers. They had nothing to report out of the ordinary. There had been a fair amount of interest in them and their vehicles but that was to be expected. No-one had tried to touch anything or take anything and there had been no sign of any threatening behaviour.

As Jean and Ruth put the children down in their cubes, Ash checked the food and environmental tests he had been running. It was bad news. He went to find Kira.

'Kira, we can't stay here. It isn't safe.'

'What do you mean?' she asked.

'Radiation levels are borderline dangerous. If we stay here any longer than the next twenty-four hours, we run the risk of developing radiation sickness.' He cast a glance in the direction of the children. 'Especially them. I think we ought to dose everyone straight away as a precaution and be on our way by morning.'

'Is it that serious? Should we leave now?'

'It is serious, but I think leaving now, abruptly and in the dark, isn't the best idea. If everyone takes the shot, we're good for twenty-four hours. If we leave in the morning, we can try and get back into signal range with the others and report in. We don't know if they've been successful or not, none of our messages seem to have gone through either. This is a bit of a dead zone.'

Kira nodded. She was bitterly disappointed that Hope wasn't the refuge she had been so sure it would be. But there was no way she was going to risk Grace's health and well-being for the sake of a few fruits and vegetables they'd somehow managed to grow but that were apparently contaminated anyway. Her stomach clenched at the thought of the food they had eaten a short while ago.

'Where are the anti-radiation meds?' she asked Ash. He pointed them out to her, she grabbed a handful and hurried over with them to her parents, Ruth and the kids.

'I have some bad news, I'm afraid,' Kira said.

'There's a surprise,' Ruth commented sourly.

'There are dangerous levels of background radiation here. We can't stay so we'll be leaving in the morning.'

Ruth paled, her eyes darting around the cavern and made to grab Sarah, acting as if she was going to make a run for it. Kira put a hand on her arm.

'It's alright Ruth, we're leaving first thing in the morning. Here, take this shot and give one to Sarah. It will protect you against the radiation.'

'Thank you, love,' said Jean. 'We'll get all the kiddies dosed up and us of course but shouldn't we leave now? I mean we know now this isn't the place, I know you had your heart set on it all and everything, but we don't want to put anyone at risk, do we? And I was saying to your father something didn't feel quite right here. I couldn't quite put my finger on it but obviously it's those people. They are all sick and they want us to stay and get sick with them. It's just, it's not right, Kira dear. Not right at all.'

'No, Mum, I know. And we are leaving but we're

185

safe here in our pods with our meds. Ash will set up a night watch and we'll leave first thing in the morning. Okay?'

Jean looked worried but nodded.

'Don't eat or drink anything else from here either, stick to our ration packs.'

'Yes, dear. Those are running low as well you know. As is my medicine. These things won't last for ever, love.'

'I know, Mum, I know. We will find you some more medicine, I promise. Try not to worry.' Kira finished giving Grace her shot and smiled fondly at the little girl who was busy trying to eat her own foot. This was her world right here, her daughter and Jed. Thinking of him hurt her chest, she missed him so much. She hoped he was safe and that he was having better luck then they were.

'Can you believe our luck?' Gloria was pacing in her rooms, Tomas and a couple of other elders were sitting in various chairs, nursing their drinks. 'This is what we need, a fresh infusion into our gene pool. This could be the answer to all our problems.'

'I think you're simplifying it a bit there, Gloria,' Tomas commented drily.

'What do you mean?'

'You can't expect a group of total strangers to jump in and start having sex with us, just because they're new. They might not even want to stay. And there are a helluva lot more men than women in that group. You can count the old woman out for starters, she isn't going to bear any more children. Which leaves Kira and the sour-faced one. Two women aren't going to help us create lots more children that quickly.'

'No but it's two new women. And all those men can mix their DNA with the viable women we have left. Our sickly children can mate with their strong ones and, and...'

'Gloria, you're talking madness. They might not even want to stay. Staying would put their health at risk. Be realistic. You know that's not a sickly gene that we're fighting here. There's radiation in the air and in the water that is slowly poisoning us.'

'And what am I supposed to do about that? Force everyone to leave their lives behind? Up-sticks and risk their safety out there? We don't know what's out there! Coalition or whatever they're calling themselves these days could be ready to pounce on us as soon as we reveal our position. Another reason why we can't let them leave.'

'I don't think you have the right to force them to stay.'

'Are you going to stand against me on this, Tomas?'

'I am. These people are looking for a fresh start. We would be offering them sickness and death.'

At that Gloria seemed to crumble from within and she half fell into a chair. 'But it's so unfair, they all look so healthy and the children...' She began to cry.

Tomas got up and put his arm around her, pulling her into his embrace. 'I know, but we have to do what's right. We cannot keep them here against their will. It makes us no better than Coalition.'

After she'd finished weeping, Gloria pulled herself together and smiled gratefully at Tomas for his support.

'Do you think they will leave in the night? Without saying goodbye?'

'I think they have more sense than that. But we may

have to catch them early in the morning, to wish them well on their journey.'

Gloria nodded and lapsed into silence, disappointed that her hopes of saving their community lay in tatters once more. She didn't want to believe that everyone who lived in Hope was so badly riddled with radiation that there was literally nothing she could do to save any of them. They would all die, gradually peter out as their immune systems gave up trying to fight the radiation sickness. Another group of humanity would be lost.

Chapter 23

'What will happen to all these people here in Hope, Ash?' Kira asked quietly. It looked like everyone in their group was sleeping or at least resting. The children were completely oblivious to any danger they might be in. They had adapted remarkably well to life on the road. It helped that they were still young enough to be easily entertained and not all that mobile. Kira dreaded to think what the journey would've been like with toddlers who wanted to walk and run all the time. It would have been impossible. She was lucky Grace wasn't walking yet but it wouldn't long.

'I'm so sorry, Kira. They're not going to make it. It could be days, weeks, even months but eventually their bodies will succumb to the background radiation levels present and they will die.' Ash hated having to tell Kira this, but he didn't want her thinking there was any way they could stay here.

'And there's nothing we can do?'

'Even if we had stockpiles of our anti-radiation medicine it wouldn't do them any good. Once they stopped taking the meds they'd be right back where they started. They are slowly poisoning themselves with the air they breathe, the water they're drinking and the food they're eating.'

Kira felt so useless. She was now grateful they hadn't taken the tour, met the rest of the community and the children. She didn't think her heart could take meeting children that she knew would be dead before the year was out.

'And we haven't put everyone at risk, have we?' she asked.

'We're lucky. We have the right meds with us, everyone is dosed up. We only ingested a small amount of food and drink and our bodies are actually pretty well equipped to deal with this stuff initially. It's the constant bombardment that becomes lethal. As long as we leave in the morning, take another dose and monitor everyone's vitals, we should be fine.'

'What if we were to take their children with us? Could we save them?'

Ash's heart broke a little as he looked at the hope in Kira's face. He shook his head. He couldn't find the words. He felt like he was letting her down, but he couldn't think about all the lives that would be lost here. This was much, much worse than the casual genocide of City 15. It explained why there had been no attempts by New Corp to investigate this settlement and extend Corp rule. The people who lived here would be dead soon enough. Why waste the resources?

The two of them sat in their misery long into the early hours of the morning, not speaking. There was nothing more either of them could think of to say. They took comfort in each other's presence and tried to focus on the next stage of their journey.

It was still dark when the operatives started to stir. No-one was going to sleep in today. The children were wide awake and full of beans, clamouring for breakfast.

Surprisingly, Ruth was taking charge today, it seemed that the brush with danger had invigorated her. She was still rather acerbic with anyone who wasn't a small child, but she had prepared breakfast for all four children and although she looked tired, today she had made an effort and brushed her hair. Kira didn't say anything directly but shared a delighted grin with her mum. They had both been worried about Ruth's general apathy and lack of desire to get involved with looking after her own baby.

There was a commotion in the entrance to the cavern as Gloria, Tomas and few other residents of Hope appeared. They looked resolute and Kira feared they would try to stop them leave.

'Good morning,' she said. 'As you can see, we are getting ready to leave. I wanted to thank you for your hospitality...'

Gloria cut her off. 'There's no need. We can see you are more technologically advanced than we are. You have probably discovered our health issues and I cannot blame you for not wanting to put yourself and your children at risk. I only wish we could have met under more pleasant circumstances.'

Kira held her hands out to the woman, who took them hesitantly. 'So you know, you know what will happen here?'

Gloria couldn't speak but she nodded once, swiftly, eyes bright, smile brittle. Kira squeezed her hands and closed her eyes in sympathy. This was so much harder than she'd thought it would be. A loud bang of a skimmer door shutting made them both jump and Kira looked to see that everyone was ready to leave. She didn't know what else to say so instead she hugged Gloria briefly and held a hand out to Tomas who shook it warmly. Ash, too, came over to formally say goodbye to the leaders of Hope but everyone else stayed in the skimmers.

Kira felt like her skin was crawling, but she knew it was only in her imagination. She'd taken the medicine; she would take the next dose and she would closely monitor her health. Everything would be fine, for them. Turning away, trying not to cry, Kira hurried to her skimmer, followed by Ash. Gloria and Tomas lifted their arms in farewell and watched in sadness as the vehicles drove out of the cavern, able to escape the doom that awaited the people left behind.

No-one spoke for a long time as the group journeyed back the way they had come. Meds were taken and they had short breaks to eat and drink from their dwindling supplies. Even the children seemed to realise that now was not the time to be fractious and they sat quietly or dozed as the countryside swept past them. Eventually the small convoy stopped for the evening and as the operatives began to set up camp, Ash began sweeping for comms messages from the other team. They had made good progress and should be back in range of some sort of comms array. Finally, he found a small, weak signal. It took a while but the message that they had been trying to send to Jed's team eventually went through and a short message from them arrived.

MESSAGE FROM TEAM 9 TO TEAM 36:
We have arrived safely and secured neural implants. We will re-con tomorrow and report back.

MESSAGE FROM TEAM 36 to TEAM 9:
Unfortunately, City 36 is non-viable, there are high levels of radiation. All of team 36 have been dosed with anti-radiation meds. We will begin the journey back

down to City 9 unless we hear differently. Hopefully your re-con will be more successful. Looking forward to getting the team back together.

Chapter 24

'Have you seen the message from the others?' Dina called out.

Everyone gathered by the comm and read the details.

'Oh, that's terrible,' said Max. 'I was hoping 36 might be a serious option for us. I thought it would be off Corporation's radar, a safe place for us.'

'No, it's completely radioactive instead. Those poor, poor people. Jed? Will the children be alright?' Martha asked urgently.

'Yes, they should be fine. As long as they took their meds and there's no way Kira would forget to do something like that.' Jed looked up at Martha and took a double take. She'd done her best to disguise her features by chopping all her hair off to a close crop and putting colour filters in her eyes to change them. 'Looks good, Ma.'

Martha flushed and smoothed her clothing apprehensively. She was fairly certain she didn't look like the ex-governor of City 42 anymore. Through internal room replicator, they'd been able to order the same jumpsuits they'd seen everyone else in the city wearing. Together with their fake neural implants, they were feeling confident that they looked the same as everyone else. It was time to test the theory.

'Everyone clear on their objective?' asked Jed.

'Checking the ocean and nosing around the docks,' replied Max.

'Getting a feel for how the city works, looking for fresh food and keeping out of the way of New Corp security patrols,' replied Dina, moving to stand next to Martha who nodded in agreement.

'Right, and I'll try and get a circuit of the city completed. See if there are any other entries or exits, any places to avoid, anything that points to the people behind City 15.'

'I think all of New Corp are responsible for that,' Dina muttered sourly as they prepared their packs.

'Did you check in with the operatives?' Jed asked her before they left.

'Yes, they are maintaining their position, outside the reach of the scanners, and have hidden their own signals so as not to raise any suspicion. If a drone flies directly over them, we won't be able to do much about it, but they've tried to use their surroundings to camouflage themselves as much as possible. They are maintaining comm silence until we report in this evening.' Dina felt a sense of pride in being able to sound so professional. Who knew she would have gone from student, to field scientist to rebel comms officer in less than a year?

They headed out of their room, trying to look as inconspicuous as possible. The two men went one way and soon split again while the women strolled off in the opposite direction.

'I suppose we should look for some breakfast or something,' suggested Martha.

'Yeah, shall we try one of these?' Dina pointed to a replicator on the corner. It was advertising nutrient

195

enhanced synth-caf, designed to set you up for a busy day ahead. It was popular, a swift moving queue had formed in front, so they joined the line. Martha felt in her pocket for tokens. When they reached the machine both women stared in dismay, it required a retinal scan to issue the drinks.

'Here, allow me.' A man pushed between them and lowered his eye to the scanner, it bleeped and pulsed green. He pressed for three and juggled them away from the dispenser. The two women followed cautiously.

'You're new in town, aren't you?' he asked as he passed the drinks over.

'What makes you say that?' Martha asked casually, trying not to sound alarmed.

'You've clearly never paid for anything here before, otherwise the retinal scan wouldn't have thrown you. And although you've done a good job, those neural implants are fake, they're not connected to the mainframe.' He took a sip of his synth-caf, watching them over the rim of his cup then grimaced at the flavour. 'Look this stuff is awful. You want some real coffee? No strings.' He held his arms out as if to show he was no threat.

Martha looked at Dina who shrugged her shoulders minutely. Both women were armed, knew how to use the stun guns, and they both had internal trackers so Jed would be able to find them if they ran into any kind of trouble. Besides there was something about this man they felt they could trust.

'Okay, lead on,' Martha replied.

'Great. I'll take those.' And he swiped the untouched synth-cafs from their hands, depositing them in the nearest refuse receptacle. With a jerk of his head he motioned for them to follow him down a nearby side street and set off a steady pace which had them scrambling to keep up. They followed the side streets for some time as the man seemed to want to keep a low profile, which was fine with them. Finally, they arrived at his destination. The building was an old red brick with an imposing black door. However, when he pushed the door open, the rich aroma of real coffee wafted out into the street. He grinned and ushered them inside.

It was a short walk down a dimly lit hallway before they came out into a kitchen. A large scarred wooden table dominated the middle of the room with various mismatched chairs arranged around the outside. There were real books, scraps of paper and pens scattered across the tabletop. A saucepan rack hung above their heads with shiny copper pans glinting in the electric lights. An old-fashioned range cooker filled one wall. It was like stepping into a history book. Then Martha noticed the plexiglass surrounding the entire scene. The man had laughter in his eyes as he beckoned them to follow him to the left. A small doorway led them into what looked like a communal restroom. There was a less interesting set up of table and chairs in here but at least they had found the source of the aroma, and it was real coffee.

'Perk of the job,' the man explained as he poured them each a cup. 'This is the city's museum, hence the impressive kitchen. But the replicators here are second to none and designed to provide the average punter with a realistic experience for their entry fee.' Martha put a hand to her pocket for tokens, but the man shook his head. 'No need.' He passed them a cup of coffee each.

Both women wrapped their hands around the hot mugs and inhaled the aroma. It felt wonderful to indulge.

'Do we stand out a lot then?' Martha asked.

'You've done a good job but for those used to looking out for non-conformers, you stick out. You're lucky you ran into me and not a security patrol. They wouldn't be giving you coffee. Where you from?'

'City 42,' Dina announced. Martha blinked at her in surprise.

'Ah. The rebel city. Although that's all finished with now. They executed quite a few dissenters up there, if you believe the sweeps of course.' He passed them a handheld.

NEWCORP: *News from City 42.*
Ben Jenkins has been terminated for crimes against the authority.
Nick Sedgwick has been terminated for crimes against the authority.
Dana Chrystal has been terminated for crimes against the authority.
Zavier Duparre, also known as ANON17, has been terminated for crimes against the authority.

Martha paled and sat down heavily on a nearby chair while Dina stifled a gasp.

'Hey, I'm sure it wasn't your fault.' The man looked worriedly at his guests. 'Look, I'm Zac. I curate the museum and I'm nosy but whatever you're doing here you don't have to worry about me reporting you to Corp Security. I keep my head down and my nose clean. I thought you looked interesting and it broke my heart to think of you drinking that synth-sludge.' He was smiling encouragingly at them.

'Thank you, Zac. I'm Martha and this is Dina. It's true we have come from City 42. We're looking for a way off the island. We had hoped that City 9 would hold the answer.'

Zac's face fell. 'I'm sorry. There's no travel out of here. The docks used to be open and we traded with some of the coastal cities across the water but when New Corp cracked down, everything stopped. We can't even get comms over there anymore. The docks have been dismantled, every boat destroyed, and the water is too poisonous to risk swimming in, although our forefathers used to enjoy a dip in the ocean - can you believe that?'

But Martha and Dina weren't listening. They had pinned their hopes on being able to get a boat and try their luck across the sea. Then Martha recalled something Zac had said.

'You said when New Corp cracked down - when was that?'

'Oof, about six months ago? I think. Things started to change, gradually at first, more in line with all things Corp. I guess we didn't notice at first and then by the time we started to question things a bit, they'd already got all their infrastructure in place and it was too late to do anything about it.' He looked at their worried faces. 'Oh, it's okay. Toe the line and you're fine. More or less the same as the previous incarnation.'

'Except for the neural implants.' Dina pointed out.

'Well yeah, they suck but there are ways to get around them - as you know.'

Max looked around with interest as he walked towards the docks. City 9 was different from City 42. It had more integrated tech and definitely had less personality. As he grew closer to the ocean, Max realised there was no way he would get to stand on the beach or obtain a sample of seawater. The area bristled with New Corp Security and there were stiff security measures along the entire length. There was also a lack of civilians in the area making him stand out. He tried to make it look as though he were looking for a person rather than access to the seashore and back tracked slightly looking for somewhere to sit and rethink his plan of action.

The food hydrators were out of the question. He'd been more observant than Martha and Dina and noticed people using the retinal scan to pay for their beverages. Instead he looked for a slightly more old-fashioned establishment, somewhere that would still take the tokens he had in his pocket. At last he found one, a small, dingy looking café with a peeling sign in the window announcing tokens still taken. Max headed in and was welcomed with the delicious odour of bread baking. Things were looking up.

It turned out they weren't quite as optimistic as he first thought, the bread aroma was fake, but he was able to buy a synth-caf and a packet of rehydrated oatmeal with his tokens. As he sat by the window Max looked out and considered his options. He hadn't seen any boats in the harbour. There was clearly no citizen access to the beach which was a cordoned off area. One reason could be that New Corp didn't want anyone leaving City 9 via the docks because it wasn't safe to travel on the water or maybe they didn't have the transportation anymore. Alternatively, they just didn't want anyone leaving City 9.

There was no sign of any fresh food available, no dock trade or fishing opportunities. It didn't even smell fishy. Max sipped his synth-caf thinking about what high levels of HER would have done to the ocean.

It may be that the acidity of the water was too much for the material boats are made of and that was why they could not make the journey across the ocean. If high levels of radiation existed within the marine life left in the ocean, they wouldn't be safe to consume so New Corp could be trying to protect their citizens by not letting them fish. It would certainly be counter-productive to allow people to slowly poison themselves.

Realising that he'd finished both his drink and breakfast, Max stood up to leave. Time to go back to the room and wait for the others. He may have disappointing news, but he hoped the rest of them had been more fortunate.

Jed tried to look as inconspicuous as possible as he walked through the city. Luckily it seemed that the citizens in City 9 did still actually walk so at least that behaviour wasn't unusual. However, everyone seemed to be highly motivated with a pre-determined purpose and Jed couldn't help wondering whether he stuck out like a sore thumb. He tried to walk with as much purpose and confidence as he could muster. It didn't help that he was feeling hungry and there didn't seem to be any shops selling food, let alone street vendors. There was the odd replicator on a street corner, but Jed didn't want to give away his ignorance by attempting to use one, especially as they all seemed busy.

City 9 was laid out in much the same grid pattern as 15 and 42 except that one edge ended in a bristling cordon, clearly the ocean lay that way. Jed continued to loop around the city, noting the walls and the power generators for the force-field. The same set up as 42. There seemed to be more a mixture of buildings here than in his city though. Corp buildings intermingled with living accommodations and it was difficult to tell whether there was a dedicated Archive or Academy presence. Jed realised that each block was a self-contained unit. The citizens of 9 lived, worked and learnt all in one area, never needing to travel elsewhere. Clearly, they were still free to walk around the city at the moment, to use the food hydrators for example, but Jed wondered how long that would last for.

The only positive thing he noticed as he walked the city's circuit were evidence of sky skimmers. There were skimmer pads located at regular intervals and some of them appeared to be citizen driven, they weren't all New Corp Security but whether any of them had clearance to leave the force-field or indeed the capability to cross the ocean from this island to the next, he did not know. Somehow, they'd have to try and find out. Hopefully there would be an info point somewhere Dina could hack.

Jed finished his circuit, feeling a little defeated that there was no obvious solution to their problem. He hoped their presence here had gone unnoticed. He had no desire to tangle with the power behind the destruction of City 15. All he wanted to do was find a safe place for himself, his family and his friends. He spotted Max walking towards him and lifted a hand in greeting. Judging by his face, he'd had as much luck as Jed.

Chapter 25

'I think we should have taken the tour,' Dina said as the two of them walked back to their room.

'Maybe, but at least this way we have an excuse to come back with Jed and Max and see if we can get a bit more information out of Zac.'

'You think he's hiding something?' Dina asked.

'I think he knows more than he's letting on and who knows, he might be able to help us in some other way.'

'You don't think he's going to report us to New Corp, do you?'

'No, I think we are safe on that front.' They arrived shortly after Max and Jed. It didn't take long for them each to share their fact-finding missions.

'We found out something else as well,' said Martha. 'It's about Ben. Jed, I'm so sorry but... he's been terminated.'

'What? How do you know that?' Jed darted his gaze between Martha and Dina.

'When we were in the museum, with Zac, he showed us the sweeps from City 42. Apparently, they've rounded up four dissenters and had them all terminated. Ben was on the list. I'm sorry, Jed.' Martha reached out an arm but Jed flinched away from it.

'I can't... this is unreal.' He looked up at Dina in disbelief. 'He said he was going to be careful. He said.'

Dina gave him a hug murmuring words of comfort. Max and Martha looked on uncomfortably until Jed recovered. With a parting squeeze he extracted himself from Dina's arms and cleared his throat loudly.

'We ought to try and let Kira know what we've found out. Dina, can you get another message out to them?' he asked.

'Their comms have been down, but now that we know they're heading back, I should be able to get through to them,' Dina replied.

Martha felt the familiar tug on her heart when they spoke about the other team. She missed Lucas.

'Send the message Dina, but keep it brief,' Jed was back to business. 'Outline the facts - no ships, high level of New Corp presence. Try to break the news about Ben as gently as you can, please.' Then he addressed the others. 'We need to come up with a different plan.'

'What about Zac?' asked Martha.

'Well, if you think he has something to hide, I'm not sure all of us heading down there will encourage him to talk,' Jed replied honestly.

'I don't think he's necessarily hiding a bad thing. I think he might be able to help us,' said Martha.

'He should certainly be able to fill in some of the blanks on the history of this city. He runs a museum for goodness' sake. The closest thing they have to Archive here. All we've found are the sweeps,' commented Max, waving a hand at the vid screen in the room. It was displaying City 9 sweeps only.

'You're both right. Shall we go back tomorrow? Try and find out more?' asked Jed.

'I think that is a great idea.' Martha was pleased, she

wanted to talk to Zac again.

There wasn't much to do other than wait for tomorrow to come. Dina had a scrambler channel running on one of their handhelds in case they heard anything from Corp Security about them or anyone matching their description. But there was nothing. And the sweeps were full of City 9 news, the usual new tech sales and gossipy pieces. In the end it lulled Martha to sleep. She was exhausted. She hadn't had any time to herself since everything had happened. She didn't feel like she'd said goodbye to Lucas properly and she missed him. She hoped it wouldn't be long before the two groups could come back together.

The next morning, they all woke early, eager to get out and do something productive. So far, coming to City 9 had only confirmed their fears and not provided them with any new ideas on what to do next.

'Do you think you'll be able to find the museum?' Jed asked.

Dina flashed her handheld at him, she'd downloaded the visitors guide from the museum yesterday. They were going primarily to talk to Zac and try and get a feel for his loyalties but at the same time she was excited to have a proper look around the museum. Kira would be so jealous.

They set off as soon as they could, there was no point in arriving too early and hanging around outside drawing attention to themselves. But when they got there, things were different from how Martha and Dina remembered them. For one the door was boarded up and the entire building had an air of neglect about it. Which not only didn't fit in with the general demeanour of the rest of the city but it certainly wasn't what the building had looked like yesterday.

'Is this the place?' Jed asked.

Martha nodded but something was definitely wrong here. She walked up to the front of the building and felt a slight resistance. She smiled then pushed her body forwards through the glamour shield that had been erected. This was old tech at its best. She supposed that Zac would only want serious visitors to his museum. Obviously, he had lowered the shield yesterday for some other reason. Either way it was ingenious. He wouldn't get bothered with people who weren't all that interested and he knew that anyone who made it through the glamour wanted to view the museum.

The others had been surprised when Martha disappeared, then Dina clapped her hands delightedly and followed before Jed or Max had chance to issue any kind of warning. The two men shrugged and followed suit. They might as well walk into the unknown together.

Past the glamour shield the building looked as it had yesterday, the front door was ajar, and an open sign could just be seen. Martha pushed the door wider and went in eagerly.

'Martha! Dina! Good to see you again.' Zac was there, standing in the atrium, arms wide in welcome. His smile slipped slightly when he clocked Max and Jed but a warm handshake from Max seemed to settle his nerves somewhat. 'I had no idea you'd be back so soon! Welcome to my little museum, guys. Tell me you're going to take the tour this time?'

'We are. Four please,' Dina said, taking charge.

'For you - no fee. Enjoy. I'll see you for coffee on the other side,' replied Zac and with a flourish he whipped back a nearby red curtain and pointed the start of the tour out to the group. With trepidation they walked through the curtain. After all, they could be walking into anything, anything at all.

It turned out to be a harmless museum of twenty-first century styled housing. Martha and Dina marvelled at how households managed with so little technology, Jed was staggered by the huge discrepancy in wages and lifestyles throughout the various echelons of society. Kira had often tried to interest him in things like this but to actually see it so vividly, in this unique setting, was much more interesting. Max walked along contentedly, it wasn't field science so it wasn't quite his thing but Dina was happy, and they seemed to be in no danger so that was his priority right now.

All too soon they came to the end of the tour and a door led them onto a small sitting area where the delicious aroma of coffee was wafting towards them.

'Is that actual coffee?' asked Jed.

Martha and Dina nodded excitedly. They had neglected to tell the others about this particular perk. Soon there was nothing but contented sighs.

'Did you enjoy my little museum, then?' Zac reappeared with a plate of biscuits that he deposited on their table, gesturing for them to help themselves. No-one needed to be asked twice. Good biscuits were like gold dust in the freezedried food supply world.

'Fascinating,' said Jed, spraying crumbs across the table. 'Sorry.'

'Really? I'm glad you think so. You don't think the front door glamour is too much, do you?'

'No, I think it's a brilliant idea - you're showing off old tech and dissuading those who aren't interested in the museum from coming in. I should imagine it's pretty difficult to keep these displays fresh and stop people from vandalising or stealing things,' replied Dina.

'It's not so bad, I have pretty good security here.'

'How much do we owe you for the entry?' asked Max, feeling in his pockets for the remainder of his tokens.

'Oh, the museum is free. They used to be free in the old world, so I figured why not.'

'How do you make any money?' pondered Martha aloud.

'Ha ha! That's easy - the wondrous gift shop. But don't worry I won't make you go in there. I get the impression you came back for more than the museum tour.' Zac's intelligent eyes swept up and down the group as he waited for someone to come clean and tell him why they were really there.

'Okay, fair enough.' Jed put down his mug. 'We want to know if you know a way out of City 9, across the ocean to the other side.'

'What makes you think the other side is better than this one?' asked Zac carefully.

'We don't. We know we can't stay here, though.'

'Four people can disappear easily enough,' countered Zac.

'There are more than four of us.'

'But you already know that,' said Martha softly. 'You know who we are, don't you? Are you going to report us?'

Zac looked at each of them in turn before slowly shaking his head.

'Yes, I know who you are, but I have no love for New Corp, and I don't agree with what they did to City 15.'

'I had no idea that the citizens here even knew about 15,' Dina commented in surprise.

'It's not common knowledge so don't expect the average drone off the street to know anything about it but there's a small group of us. Disconnected from the neural network. Not loyal to New Corp and just trying to keep our heads above water. We don't have weapons or a way of fighting back but we do have information and we help where we can.'

'You'll help us, then?' Jed wanted to make sure this guy was on the same page. He didn't know why exactly, but he didn't trust Zac yet. There might be an answer to their problems here, there might not.

'You can't leave City 9 by boat. They don't exist anymore. Besides the seawater is too toxic for any kind of material to spend any length of time on there.'

Max nodded to himself, exactly what he had thought.

'You might be able to do it by air. I know someone who runs a private airstrip. He might be convinced to fly you over the water to the nearest safe zone, but it won't be cheap. I hope you have more than tokens to offer.'

Martha looked at Jed, she didn't think they had anything of any value at all to offer but this guy might be their only option.

'We'll get whatever it is he wants,' she replied confidently. 'But we need to get in touch with our other party first.'

'There are more of you, here in the city?' Zac sounded surprised.

'No.' Martha didn't elaborate. She didn't want to put Zac into any further danger by telling him more than he needed to know.

Zac nodded to himself. Trust worked both ways, he was well aware of that. 'Look, I think we should get you out of the city at least. You've been lucky so far, but New Corp Security patrols are getting more and more invasive. It won't take them long to figure out who you are when you fail the retinal ident scan. I'm assuming you haven't registered your irises in the city's mainframe?'

There were faint no's and head shakes.

'Look, it's not all bad. I can take you to an abandoned outpost nearby, you can get in touch with whoever you need to and then when you're ready, get in touch with me. I'll take you to Artem. He'll come up with some mad plan to get you out of here - for a price - everybody wins. What do you say?' Zac looked at them, his face so open and honest that the group couldn't help but trust and believe him.

'Sounds like a plan,' Jed replied.

'Do you have any gear with you?' Zac asked.

'It's in our room,' replied Martha.

'Now that is risky, patrols can search public shared space without regard to whether guests are present or not. It's probably best if I go and collect your things.'

'Now wait a minute, we've done alright so far,' Jed protested.

'Yes, but every time you go out there, your face gets ident scanned hundreds of times from every camera, every model citizen, every food replicator. Believe me, if the powers that be don't know you are here, they will soon.'

'Okay fine, then let me come with you at least. Leave the others here to lie low. I know where everything is that we need. We didn't leave it lying around, you know. We have some common sense.' Jed's pride was a little hurt, this wasn't his first mission, he wasn't a rookie.

Zac nodded. 'Okay, but do me a favour, wear this and try not to look at anything.' He threw a baseball cap at Jed who caught it in surprise.

'Won't this make me stick out even more?'

'Not today, it's games day and everyone will be wearing one, trust me.' Zac stood up. 'Let's get moving, shall we? Game time is the perfect time to get you out of the city without being noticed.'

Jed stood and put the cap on his head, he hoped trusting Zac was the right thing to do. They were putting an awful lot of trust into a stranger's hands. The others helped themselves to more coffee as they waited for Jed and Zac to come back.

The two men were able to stroll through the city unnoticed. Zac had been right; they didn't stick out at all. It seemed like all the citizens of City 9 were out in force, all clad with different coloured baseball hats. It was surreal.

'How is this happening?' asked Jed in a low voice.

'People get attached to the strangest things and no matter how hard Corp or even New Corp tried with their neural implants, they couldn't get rid of the love of the game,' explained Zac.

'Huh.'

Jed entered their room cautiously, but nothing looked out of place. 'I guess Security haven't been by yet.'

'Yeah, you probably got lucky with it being game day. We should hurry. Whilst we don't stick out at the moment, once everyone has gone into the stadium we will.'

Jed nodded and went through the room briskly. Fortunately, they had been neat and consistent with where they had placed their things and it didn't take long to gather everything together. Back on the street they did look slightly out of place carrying three bags each, especially as the crowds were thinning with the game about to start. But they managed to make it back to the museum without incident. They did see one security patrol, but the three guards were so involved in ribbing the fourth man with them on his choice of team, they didn't even see Jed and Zac.

'What's the plan now?' asked Max, once everyone had been reunited.

'We've got about ninety minutes until the end of game time. Everyone will be piling out then, that's the best time to leave the city. You should have something to eat, get some rest. We'll have to move fast once the game finishes. Curfew,' Zac replied.

'Are you coming with us?' asked Martha.

'Well, I'll have to take you past the city wall. You'll need a local in case you run into a patrol. After that, it's up to you but, if you'll take me, I'll come with you.'

The others said nothing. This was an unexpected development. The silence dragged on uncomfortably until Zac coughed and stood.

'I'll, er... let you talk amongst yourselves.' And he left the room.

'What do you think?' Martha asked the others.

'Do you think he's some kind of spy? For New Corp, I mean?' asked Dina.

'I know what you mean. I don't know. He's been truthful with us so far. And let's face it, how long will he survive in a city that clearly only wants biddable, controlled citizens while he's running a museum that celebrates a way of life wiped out two hundred years ago?' Martha felt she would know if Zac were a spy. Just because Sean had completely hoodwinked her back in 42 didn't mean she had lost all judgement. Besides, she rather liked Zac. It would be nice to have another person to talk to.

'I don't think he's a spy for New Corp, but I don't think he's told us everything he knows,' Max volunteered.

'After everything that's happened, I don't know whether we can afford to trust anyone new. And I'm not keen on taking a stranger with us when we go to meet with the others. Those are our children we are potentially putting at risk,' said Jed.

'It doesn't seem fair of us to discount Zac after all the help he's giving us here in City 9. We would have been identified and contained by now for sure.' Martha tried to argue her case.

'Possibly, possibly not. Are you ready to take the risk, Martha?'

'Look, where are we going to lead him? To two skimmers hidden on the outskirts of the city where ten fully armed, fully trained operatives will be on hand to detain him if necessary.'

Jed nodded. He had already executed that plan in his mind. If Zac came with them, he would be swept for bugs, tagged and more than likely magno-bound under armed guard until Jed could prove one way or another whether he was with them or against them.

'We'd better put him out of his misery, otherwise he might decide to defect and alert New Corp to us being here in City 9,' Dina joked weakly.

Martha glared at her as she went to tell Zac the good news.

ENCRYPTED MESSAGE FROM CITY 9 TO CITY 42
>>*Martha Hamble, Dina Grey & Jed Jenkins plus one other have visited the City 9 museum twice. This confirms our suspicions that the museum is linked to the Resistance - why else would they visit it twice?* <<

ENCRYPTED MESSAGE FROM CITY 42 TO CITY 9
>>SEND A STRIKE FORCE IN TO RETRIEVE ANY DATA AND THEN REPURPOSE THE BUILDING. DETAIN FOR QUESTIONING ANY CITIZENS. ANY SIGHTINGS OF KIRA JENKINS OR RUTH MADDOCKS?<<

ENCRYPTED MESSAGE FROM CITY 9 TO CITY 42
>>*No, although a communication was intercepted originating from Hamble's base here in City 9. We have been unable to decode the message but it was tagged for Team 36.*<<

ENCRYPTED MESSAGE FROM CITY 42 TO CITY 9
>>THEY MUST HAVE SPLIT UP AND SENT THE OTHERS UP TO CITY 36. EXCELLENT, RADIATION LEVELS ARE TOXIC IN THE NORTH. SHOULD YOU INTERCEPT ANY MORE COMMUNIQUES, REPORT THEM IMMEDIATELY<<

Chapter 26

Zac led Jed and the others to a disused service hatch. It exited outside the city, unaffected by the force and was unguarded. By the time New Corp Security arrived at Zac's museum, there was no-one there to apprehend. On their journey from the city limits out to camp, Zac's handheld beeped frantically.

'What's that?' asked Dina.

Zac looked at his screen in dismay. 'New Corp have breached the museum. They're trying to download my servers, but they triggered the self-destruct.'

'Will they know where we've gone?' asked Jed.

Zac answered distractedly as he flicked through his handheld. 'No, no, they won't be able to get hold of any of my files. It's fine.' He kept going until he found what he was looking for, then he looked up at the others. 'That's that then. The museum is gone.'

Martha patted his shoulder in commiseration while the others expressed their sorrow. They continued the journey to the skimmers in silence. On arrival, Jed went to check in with the operatives, so Dina, Martha and Max took Zac over to the communal tent. The largest of their temporary structures, it housed the shared food supplies, a travel hydrator and a synth-caf machine.

There were no tables, they were too bulky to pack and only a handful of fold away chairs.

'We haven't got much but help yourself to a hot drink, whatever you need. No coffee though, I'm afraid. Will you be alright here for a moment?' asked Martha.

Zac nodded and busied himself making a synth-caf while the others went to find Jed. He was checking the comms system.

'Listen, there's a message from Kira,' Jed said and he read it aloud. 'I didn't think 9 would have what we need, New Corp are too prevalent. I can't believe Ben is gone - Mum is in bits. I dread to think what would have happened to us if we'd stayed. We're about a day away, see you all soon.'

'At least they've made good time,' commented Max. 'It'll be good to have everyone in one place.'

'I can't wait to see Lucas and the other children,' said Martha. 'I hope he's alright.'

'I'm sure he's fine, Ma. But what about Zac? Are we magno-binding him?' asked Dina. 'He just lost his entire livelihood and I can't help but think it's because he was helping us.'

'No, we won't bind him,' replied Jed. 'But he stays away from the armoury and the comms system. And he doesn't leave camp without an escort.'

'Are you talking about me, by any chance?' Zac asked with a smile, which slipped as no-one said anything. 'Um, do you want me to go away?'

'Actually, what can you tell us about this Artem? I assume you managed to make contact?' asked Jed.

'Yes, I sent him a message. He has his own airstrip which is about half a day's journey from here. We should be welcome to stay on his estate for as long as we need to, he enjoys having visitors,' replied Zac.

'And he's definitely not loyal to New Corp?' asked Martha.

'No, definitely not.'

Martha smiled encouragingly and took Zac back with her to the communal tent while the others drifted apart to see to their own errands. Jed felt like he wouldn't be able to relax until he was reunited with Kira, Grace and Peter. He missed them all fiercely and he couldn't wait to get to know Peter better. In order to distract himself, Jed checked on the camp security. He didn't want to be surprised by any New Corp drones.

'I get the impression the others don't trust me very much,' Zac said to Martha as they strolled through the grassy verge next to the road.

'It's not that they don't trust you, they don't know you. I don't know you.' She smiled at him, to show that she didn't mean it in a negative way.

'I'm just me. There's not much to tell.'

'I'm listening.' Martha linked an arm through Zac's and waited patiently. She was desperate for him to open up to her so she could prove the others wrong; that Zac was trustworthy, and they had been right to bring him with them on their journey.

'Well, I was grown in 9. They have a small baby lab, but most children came from 42 until you closed down that operation. My parents are both dead, resisters to various Corp initiatives.'

'Sorry,' whispered Martha, feeling guilty. She hadn't considered the ramifications of their actions before. Not knowing what the other cities nearby were like had made it difficult to consider the possibility that her actions would have negative consequences for others.

'It's okay, it happened a long time ago - way before your coup, but that did lead to a major crackdown by the way. The museum belonged to my parents. Naturally I lived there, so I sort of carried on running the place. It does, did, alright. People, if nothing else, are pretty curious about things that have gone before. I was regularly checked by New Corp Security to make sure I wasn't planning any additional nefarious activity.'

'Bit of a risk to throw everything in with us, then.'

'Yes and no. There is nothing left in 9 for me. My business has been destroyed and apart from wearing a fake neural transmitter there's not much resistance one person can achieve, provided he doesn't want to end up instantly detained.'

'I suppose not.' Martha paused, trying to find the right words. 'But you have helped others, haven't you?'

Zac nodded but said nothing.

'Are you Anti-Corp?'

'What's Anti-Corp?' he asked.

'It's what the organisation was called in City 42 that opposed Corporation. I thought you might have heard of it,' Martha explained.

'No, there's no Anti-Corp.' Zac stopped walking and looked directly into Martha's eyes. 'We're the Resistance.'

A thrill leapt through her body. 'I knew it! I knew you were hiding something.'

'Well, I had to make sure it was safe before I could tell you,' said Zac.

'You had to make sure it was safe before you could tell us?' Martha laughed. 'You do know who we are, right?'

Zac chuckled. 'I know, but you can never be too careful.' He got serious. 'New Corp will be after us both now.'

'And your friend, Artem, he can help us?'

'I hope so.' They lapsed into silence and walked on like that for a few minutes until Zac revived the conversation. 'What about you, anyway - what's your background?'

'Well, my father was on the Board in City 42 so I'm a made to order.'

'Wow, that's rare these days.'

'Yep, that's me. No siblings.'

'Hang on, your father was on the Board? What does he do now? Did he defect as well? Is that how you managed such a successful coup?'

'He was murdered. He was helping us but things got out of hand and he was in the way.' Martha's voice wobbled a little.

'Oh, frag, I'm so sorry.'

'It's alright, I've come to terms with it - more or less. After mob rule got rid of the Corporation Board the city officials made me governor and I did the best I could. It was hard not having access to the Corporation mainframe and their systems. I guess we never considered the amount of behind the scenes organisation that goes into running a city. Plus, there was Lucas.'

'Lucas?'

'Yes, I'm a mum.' Martha waited on tenterhooks to see what kind of reaction Zac would display.

'Huh.' That was all he said. 'Assignment?'

'Nope.'

'Huh.' He looked a little stunned but as he didn't ask any further questions, Martha decided not to volunteer any additional information. She glanced at him, but he wasn't looking in her direction. She tucked her hair behind her ears and checked again. This time he caught her eye and gave her a brief smile.

They lapsed into a comfortable silence, each

thinking about what the other had told them. Both had questions but neither was ready to quiz the other yet. It was getting dark when they returned to the communal tent and helped themselves from the dwindling supply of dried rations, joining the others.

'When the other team arrive, we'll pool our supplies, rest for one more evening and then head out to your contact, Zac,' said Jed. 'I assume they will be able to help us out on the supplies front?'

'Shouldn't be a problem but I warn you, Artem doesn't give anything away for free. There will be some kind of price.'

'We have a supply of tokens - would that be enough?' Dina wondered.

Zac's mouth twisted a little. 'It's not normally that kind of price.' He looked up at the others. 'Look, I don't know what he's going to say. He can help us, but... I can't even begin to guess what the fee will be. I'll do everything in my power to keep it reasonable. He's a good guy, he's just a better businessman.'

Jed stewed on this for a while. Besides their dwindling rations which they needed to increase, not give away, they didn't have anything of any value they could trade. This was beginning to look like it could be a problem. At least he had an up to date inventory list now, surely, they would be able to barter something. All he had to do was wait one more day.

ENCRYPTED MESSAGE FROM CITY 42 TO CITY 9
>>DID YOU APPREHEND THEM?<<

ENCRYPTED MESSAGE FROM CITY 9 TO CITY 42
>>No, they escaped. Hamble and the others have met up with the rest of their group. There was some kind of illegal computer programme running at the museum so we have terminated it.<<

ENCRYPTED MESSAGE FROM CITY 42 TO CITY 9
>>GOOD. DO YOU KNOW WHERE THEY ARE GOING NOW?<<

ENCRYPTED MESSAGE FROM CITY 9 TO CITY 42
>>There's only one place they can go. Artem Misner's enclosure is the only populated place left.<<

ENCRYPTED MESSAGE FROM CITY 42 TO CITY 9
>>DO WE HAVE EYES?<<

ENCRYPTED MESSAGE FROM CITY 9 TO CITY 42
>>Of course.<<

ENCRYPTED MESSAGE FROM CITY 42 TO CITY 9
>>CONTINUE TO MONITOR AND REPORT REGULARLY. LET'S GET AS MANY DISSIDENTS AS POSSIBLE IN ONE PLACE BEFORE ORDERING THE STRIKE<<

Chapter 27

Kira was frantic. Grace had started crying in the night and then she'd vomited everywhere. It had been stressful trying to soothe Grace while at the same time strip her off, wash her, get clean clothes, clean up the mess, try not to wake the others, which of course didn't work, and then listen to Grace scream inconsolably as Kira quickly changed and washed herself. She was now sitting upright with her poorly little girl snuggled into her chest. Grace had been sick three times and was running a high fever. She wouldn't take anything except for the tiniest sips of water.

'Why is she so poorly?' Kira asked her mum, but Jean shook her head.

'Children get sick, my lovely. Do you remember burning up with that temperature when you were little? Came out of nowhere, it did. Caught us all by surprise, one minute you were playing happily with your toys, the next you were a droopy, crying little thing. Didn't take you long to throw up everywhere - I never could get the smell out of the old cloth doll you had. Had to throw that away we did, didn't we, Malcolm? Oh, he's asleep. Bless him, he can sleep through most anything. But I wouldn't worry, my love, it'll be a stray sickness bug she's picked up. Could've got it from anywhere. Children do, you know. It's because they're so inquisitive, they love to poke things and prod things and put them in their mouths. It's a wonder any of us make it to adulthood, it really is.' She caught the panicked expression on her daughter's face. 'Honestly, love, she'll be fine - you'll see. It's a twenty-four-hour bug. You gave her some medicine, didn't you? Keep offering her fluids and don't let her temperature get too high and she'll be fine. It's sleep she needs now. That's a great healer.'

'But what if she's really ill? What if she's got radiation poisoning from that stupid cave? I should never have taken her in there. I could've killed her!' Kira was on the verge of tears.

'Now listen to me, young lady. You haven't killed your little girl, she's right there on your knee. Sleeping peacefully and looking like an angel, if I might add. That's silly talk, that is. We all went into the caves and Grace is the only one who is poorly and yes, I know, we are bigger than her, but the other small ones are all fine. It could be anything that has caused this. Anything. She might have been harbouring a bug for a couple of days. It's not your fault. Children get sick. Mark my words, she'll be right as rain tomorrow.'

Kira sniffed, feeling useless but trying to take comfort from her mum's words. She had run the radiation wand over Grace, and the other children, several times and it had never alarmed or even come back with any kind of warning reading. Not even borderline. They hadn't stayed at the caves long enough. But her baby girl was ill. And Kira didn't know why. She gently tucked a curl behind Grace's ear and held her close.

By the time morning arrived, Grace had been sick

twice more and Kira was at her wits' end. She wasn't taking in any advice her mum was trying to give and had decided to use the skimmer's inbuilt refuse system to incinerate all the blankets that they'd used to mop up the vomit, so frightened that she was going to infect everyone else. Luckily, they did have a few spare ones, but if Grace continued to be sick, some of the adults would be going cold tonight.

Fortunately, Kira wasn't needed for any kind of driving duty. Instead, she barricaded herself and Grace into the rear of the second skimmer, the one which carried most of the equipment, and only allowed one operative in to drive the vehicle. He was instructed to stay firmly behind the plexiglass window which was not to be lowered under any circumstances. She also ordered Ash to tell Jed what had happened. He wanted to intervene, but Jean told him to let Kira get on with it.

'The poor dear is scared witless. Nothing we say will get through to her. Let her be with her little one and she'll soon see that everything will be alright. Make sure she's got lots of disinfectant in there with her so the bugs don't leap from the child to the grown up and everything will be fine. The last thing we want is for Kira to start vomiting as well.'

Ash left her to it and went to check on Ruth before he sent a message to Jed. He found her with Lucas, Sarah and Peter.

'Are you okay, Ruth? Can I get you anything?'

'A bit more space would be good,' Ruth joked with a smile. She and the children had been squashed into the first skimmer with Kira's parents. Luckily most of the operatives were happy to walk alongside and they'd been able to maintain a steady pace.

Ash nodded and went to make sure they would still

make their rendezvous with Jed and the others. Despite Grace's sickness, he didn't want them to be late. The rest of the journey went smoothly, and by the time they reached the other group, Kira was passed out exhausted in her designated sick bay. Little Grace was sleeping off the tail end of her sickness.

Martha rushed to be reunited with Lucas and was hugging Ruth and Sarah, so pleased to see them both again. Dina and Max were entertaining Peter, making him giggle whilst Ash gave Jed a brief report.

'Once we left Hope there were no issues, apart from...' Ash trailed off.

'Thanks, Ash. I'll go see her now.' Jed was concerned by Kira's behaviour and had been worried ever since receiving Ash's message. He gave Peter a quick kiss on the head before he hurried to the skimmer.

The rest of the operatives had gone into Jed's makeshift camp with all the supplies they could carry. They would put all their resources together and get an idea as to whether they had anything worth trading when they went to see Artem. Zac wandered over and started chatting with Ash about tech before Martha brought over Lucas, Ruth and Sarah and the conversation changed to cooing over the children. Whilst Zac and Ruth were chatting, Martha spoke to Jean.

'Ruth seems better,' she said.

'She's come on leaps and bounds, love. It was that scare in those caves that did it, I think. A proper brush with death, if you like. Realised she can't go on without caring about life and the people in it. Knows she needs to be there for her little one, she does. It's difficult times we live in, Martha. Difficult times.'

They both turned their gaze to the skimmer where Kira was.

225

'Do you think I ought to go see if she's alright?' asked Martha.

'Let Jed see to her, love. You introduce me to this new young man and tell me all about your adventures,' said Jean, taking Martha's mind off her friend.

Jed eased the door to the skimmer open and Kira's eyes flew open in panic. The stale smell of old vomit and unwashed bodies hit Jed in the face, and he had to take a moment before he could continue.

'NO! Don't come in. It's not safe,' Kira cried out.

'Kira, love. It's me. It's Jed.'

'Jed? Did we make it already? Is that you? Oh Jed, Grace is sick. She's really, really sick and I don't know what to do.'

'Alright love, let me take her. Come on. It's alright. I've got her.' Jed reached in and extracted his daughter from Kira's arms. The little girl felt a little warm, but Jed was sure that was from having been held by her mum for hours on end. He used the handheld scanner Max had given him and swept it over their daughter. Kira waited on tenterhooks for the resulting beep.

'Well?' she asked.

'She's fine. No bugs. No radiation. A little dehydrated but we can sort that out. Now let's check you.'

'No, no, I'm fine. I need to be there for her in case, in case...' Kira wilted under Jed's stern gaze. 'Okay, let's do me.'

He ran the scanner again. 'Well, no sign of infection but like Grace you're dehydrated and are suffering from exhaustion.' He grinned at his wife. 'You also stink. I'm sending you to the wash pod.'

Kira looked at him, momentarily overwhelmed by everything that had happened. She began to cry.

'Hey, hey, love. It's alright. It's okay. Grace is okay. You're okay. We're back together and everything is going to be alright. Come on, out you get of the stink mobile.' And Jed helped his wife out of the skimmer, supporting her wobbly legs as she took in the sight of everyone back together again.

'I do stink, don't I?' Kira asked.

'Yes, you do.'

'And Grace is going to be alright?'

'Yes, love. She is.'

Kira allowed herself to be led to the wash pod and hugged her husband gratefully before going inside and getting clean. It was probably the most awkward piece of kit they'd had to carry with them, but easily the most appreciated. Jed went in search of his mother-in-law to put his daughter into safe hands and to find some clean clothes for Kira.

Dina and Max were filling Ruth in on their adventures, while she was trying to simultaneously tell them about everything that had happened to her group. Martha and Zac had taken over the rations check and were trying to put together some sort of meal everyone could share - it was going to be a bit hit and miss but at least they were all together. The two teams of operatives were greeting each other like long lost family and bragging about the things they'd seen. No-one knew what they would be walking into tomorrow when they went to see Artem. Even Zac hadn't been able to offer up much in the way of information, which bothered Jed.

But for now, for tonight, it was about the group being back together; reconnecting and sharing their stories. Jed looked down fondly at Peter and Grace playing together. It was a time for family bonding.

Chapter 28

'So, Zac, where exactly is this compound?' asked Jed, once the evening meal had finished and the children were all in bed.

'I don't exactly know...'

'I thought you said it was some kind of huge mansion or something. It's got a runway - how can you not know where it is?' Dina was incredulous.

Zac shrugged and laughed nervously. 'I've never actually met him.'

'What?' Jed grabbed Zac's arm. 'You've never even met him?' He glared at the man, fighting the urge to punch him. 'Do you work for New Corp?'

'No!' Zac wrenched his arm out of Jed's grip. 'I would never work for them.' He was breathing heavily now, and the two men stood toe to toe, both on the verge of violence.

'Hey, what's going on?' Somehow Kira slid herself between the two of them, forcing them both to back down.

'He doesn't even know this Artem guy. He's never met him. We could be walking into anything.' Jed turned his anger onto his wife. 'Are you ready to risk your family's safety on some random bloke's word?'

'That's not fair, Jed. Calm down.' Kira turned away from her husband, ignoring him for the moment. 'Zac, please explain.'

Zac huffed a little and darted his eyes around, but there was no consolation for him. Everyone was blank faced, watching, waiting to hear what he had to say. He looked at the floor and scuffed his shoes.

'Zac?' Martha's voice was soft yet pleading.

'I have never met Artem, but I have sent others, like you, to him and he helps people. He's on the side of the Resistance but he always has a price. I can't tell you what that will be except that it's not tokens. He doesn't need them.' Zac focused on Martha, she alone seemed sympathetic to him. 'He contacted me through my museum years ago. He was impressed with my collection, even donated some bits over the years.'

'And what did he ask for in return?' asked Jed.

'He has, had, a plug-in to my network port. It was untraceable but it allowed him access to the city's sweeps, so he knows what New Corp is up to. We can trust him,' replied Zac.

'Oh, we can, can we?' Jed didn't sound convinced and walked away, signalling to his operative team leaders. He wanted to review the security protocols again. He was not going to be caught out unawares.

The rest of the group quickly broke up, leaving Martha and Zac on their own.

'Why didn't you tell us you didn't know Artem?' asked Martha.

'I didn't think it was important. I trust the guy; I thought my word would be enough. Obviously not.'

'Don't blame Jed, he's been through a lot recently. We all have. And...' She paused, uncertain how to continue.

229

'And?'

Martha flushed. 'We don't really know you, Zac. We're putting a lot on faith here. I mean, you're only with us because I vouched for you.'

'Yeah, thanks.' Zac walked away, hands in his pockets. An operative peeled away from camp to follow him while Martha looked on helplessly. Deciding there was nothing more she could say, she went to find the others who were sitting together discussing what would happen tomorrow.

'This Artem guy, have you got a last name?' asked Ruth.

'Yeah, it's Artem Misner I think,' replied Martha, sitting down to join them with a cup of synth-caf. 'Why?'

'Misner... Misner... I think I know him,' mused Ruth.

'Ha! You think you know everyone,' said Kira, making the group laugh.

'Yeah but Misner, that's distinctive isn't it? I'm sure I've heard it somewhere before.' Ruth trailed off.

'Is Zac okay?' Dina asked Martha.

'Yeah I think so. Frustrated that he doesn't know more, I think. He wants to help us. It's not his fault he's never been to the complex before.'

'Aha!' shouted Ruth, making everyone jump. 'I know where I know him from. We were, er... friends, back in the early Anti-Corp days.' She was blushing slightly. 'If it's the same Artem then he's definitely on our side. I didn't realise he'd done so well for himself.'

'Yeah, how does one person end up with their own runway, mansion and secure complex?' asked Dina.

'Luck?' suggested Martha.

'More like a combination of smuggling, connections and other illegal dealings,' replied Jed. 'The sort of person I would usually be locking up not running to for help.' He checked his wristplant. 'It's getting late, we ought to try and get some rest. It's an early start in the morning.'

The others murmured agreement and went off to bed. Kira yawned sleepily as she checked on Grace then sighed heavily, getting into bed with her husband.

'How did we get here, Jed?'

'What do you mean, love?'

'We're fugitives, on the run because the spirit of the Earth showed herself to us and asked for help. We're about to go beg some rogue to grant us passage across the ocean to who knows what and New Corp could probably wipe us all out at any minute. I don't know whether to be excited or scared.'

'I feel the same, but we can't stop now. And we can't go back.'

'I know. I wish we had some reassurances that we were doing the right thing,' said Kira as she snuggled into her husband's arms and drifted into sleep. A bee buzzed lazily around their heads before bumbling out across the camp.

The next morning Zac joined them all for breakfast. 'I've received the coordinates for Artem.' He passed his handheld over to Ash who input them into one of the skimmer's pads that he had with him.

'Hmm, not far. Looks like it will take a couple of hours. I'll go tell the team.' Ash handed it back to Zac and with a nod from Jed walked over to the operatives milling in camp. He began to round them up. It wouldn't take long for them to pack away the makeshift camp and be ready to move out.

'Right, let's get ready to go then.' Jed rubbed his hands together and stood up. The rest of them followed, gathering nearby bits and bobs so nothing was left behind. By the time the children were all strapped into the skimmer, everyone was ready, so the group moved out.

Ash was right. It only took a couple of hours to get to Artem's complex. And when they arrived, they were met with a closed fence, armed guards and vicious looking dogs.

Chapter 29

'Halt! State your business!' shouted one of the security guards.

Jed motioned for Zac to exit the skimmer and come with him to speak to the guard. They walked forward cautiously, Zac eyeing the rifles nervously. As they neared the fence, Jed gave Zac a little nudge of encouragement. He gulped and took half a step forward.

'Er... it's me. Zac, Zac Ridgley. Um, I'm here to see Artem? He sent me the coordinates. He should be expecting me, um, us I mean.'

There was a tense pause as the guard spoke into his wristplant and they all waited for a response.

'Da.' The guard nodded in their direction. '*Otkryt' vorota*!'

Before Jed had chance to ask Zac what that meant the gates started to open. The two men scrambled back to the skimmer as the vehicles then drove into the armed complex.

'This Artem guy is serious, huh?' Dina mused as they looked out the window at the gates closing swiftly behind them.

Nobody responded as the vehicles followed the gravel driveway that led up to an impressive looking house. The entire roof was covered with solar panels and antennae of various shapes and sizes. Huge generators sat on either side of the building and a single figure stood on the steps to greet them. He was a tall, powerfully built man with a buzz cut and chiselled jaw.

'That's Artem,' said Zac as everyone prepared to leave the vehicles. Kira, Martha and Ruth gathered up their children while Dina took Peter. Jed, Ash, Max and Zac went first, leaving Jean and Malcolm bringing up the rear. Jed had already ordered the operatives to stay with the skimmers until they had established their position here.

'Zac!' Artem started to walk down the steps with his arms held wide. 'You made it, my friend. So good to see you.' As he grew closer, he held out his hand and grabbed one of Zac's, pumping it enthusiastically. His gaze roamed across the group, taking in the children and the operatives beyond. Then he did a double take. 'Ruthie?'

Ruth flushed and nodded, shifting Sarah to a more comfortable position on her hip.

'RUTHIE!' Artem roared and tried to crush her in a bear hug. The loud noise and commotion made Sarah cry which caused Lucas and then Grace follow suit. Peter looked on seriously. 'Oh *rebyonochek*, *rebyonochek*. Hush, hush now, I am sorry little one.' Artem half shrugged apologetically as the mothers soothed the babies. 'Come. Come into house. We will have wine. And talk!' He swung his body round and threw an arm around both Zac and Ruth's shoulders. 'My Zac and my Ruthie! What a day, what a day.' He steered them up the stairs and into his home. The rest of the group followed behind.

On entering, various staff members bustled around

them, taking jackets and ushering them sideways into a reception room which had been prepared for them. There were wash bowls and towels, water and fruit juice to drink and an array of snacks - fresh fruit, biscuits, crackers, smoked sausage and even some chocolate. Dina walked forward enthusiastically but Kira held her back from approaching the food. She remembered what had happened in City 36.

Artem had let go of Zac and Ruth and turned to see why no-one was helping themselves. 'What? You no like? You want something different?' A puzzled look upon his face.

'It's not that, it looks lovely, so generous of you. It's just... is it safe? What are your radiation levels like?' asked Kira.

'My radiation levels? Ha! You funny lady. There is no radiation here - this safe place. Please eat, eat!' Artem gestured wildly at the table.

It was all they needed. Jed sent Ash back to the skimmers to tell the operatives to come through and have something to eat. Everyone else hurried forward, chattering excitedly and exclaiming over each new morsel they discovered. Once they satisfied their initial hunger the team relaxed, sitting around the room with plates of food and a drink, waiting to see what would happen next. Ruth went to sit next to Artem, having left Sarah with her Auntie Jean.

'Ruthie. My Ruthie. Life shines on you, eh?' Artem nodded towards the baby.

'Sort of. You know she's natural?'

'I know. I get all sweeps.' Artem spread his arms expansively. 'Corp fart and I know. Hahaha!'

'Why haven't they tried to stop you?' asked Jed.

'I pay. They leave me alone to do what I do, and I

235

pay. Always a greedy man at top. Always wanting something, I get something.' Artem shrugged as if it were no big deal.

'They could wipe you out if they wanted to then,' said Jed, feeling defeated.

'No, no, no, no, no. Is not happening. I have antennae. I get all sweeps. I am network. No-one breathes, I don't know.' Seeing that Jed looked unconvinced Artem started to point the people dotted around the room.

'Her - Dina. Lost family in 15 riots, very sad. Lost baby. Very, very sad. Work in Camp Eden. Now here.' He moved on. 'Him, Dr Max. Him big scientist fella. He discover Earth, she heal. This is good. Good work.' Artem nodded in satisfaction as people began paying attention to what he was saying. 'You. You Jean and Malcolm. You lovely peoples. You look after and you talk. Jabber, jabber, jabber. Hahaha!'

Everyone was smiling but he wasn't finished.

'You. You Ashvin - you big time techie. You come see my system. You learn.' The finger moved on. 'You Martha Hamble, you governor, important lady. Special lady, special baby.' His eyes misted slightly. 'Much loves. And you! You Kira and Jed. Importants people. You are seeing her, blue lady. Gaia.'

He sat back in satisfaction.

'What about me then?' asked Ruth in an amused voice.

'You're my Ruthie. Is enough.'

Zac coughed, feeling a little miffed at being ignored. Artem huffed at him and waved a hand. 'You Zac. Everyone know Zac. Is good.'

Jed put his plate down on the floor. 'Well, you clearly know who we are. Who are you?'

All eyes swivelled back to Artem. He leant back in his chair and began speaking, using his hands expansively.

'Me, I am Artem. I listen and I collect and I pay. Corporation they no see what I do. Some peoples come to me and I help. I have plane. Is enough.'

'So, will you help us?' asked Jed.

There was a tense moment until Artem clapped his hands. 'Of course! I help you and you show me blue lady. Come. I bring room.'

Kira shared a worried look with Jed. None of them had the power to make Gaia appear. She hadn't seen her in weeks and apart from the one dream, there had hardly been any contact. The group dutifully followed Artem back into the large foyer of his house and began to ascend the grand staircase. He showed them to the guest wing, containing enough bedrooms for them all, including dorm rooms with bunks for all the operatives.

'You rest. Have shower. Take moment. We will talk more at dinner.' And he left them to their own devices.

Jed cleared his throat. 'Well, I guess we'll all take a shower then. Ash, can you organise Alpha and Beta team to get their gear sorted out? I want everyone to take the opportunity for a wash and a rest.' He waited while Ash jogged back to the team to relay the message before turning back to the others. 'See you back here in an hour?'

Everyone nodded and went through to their respective rooms.

'What do you think about Artem?' Kira asked her husband.

'He's certainly a character.'

'Should we be worried that he pays New Corp to leave him alone?'

'It must be a fragging big pay out for them to turn a blind eye to all this.' Jed gestured around. 'The man is an information nexus. He must have something on everyone. I can't believe it's tokens that keep them away.'

'Do you think he will help us?'

'I think if he finds us interesting enough then yes, he'll help us.'

'Well,' said Kira. 'We'd better be extremely interesting at dinner then.' And she hurried off to get freshened up.

When everyone was ready, they reconvened and made their way downstairs, following the delicious aromas to the dining room where Artem was waiting for them. There was one long table for the operatives and a smaller one with four highchairs Artem had produced from somewhere. Everyone sat looking forward to a delicious meal.

As staff served the first course of some kind of vegetable broth, Dina spoke up. 'Where do you get your produce, Artem?'

'I grow and I buy. Is not hard. Always something for something,' he replied.

Everyone tucked in, the children playing with breadsticks.

As the soup bowls were cleared away and a simple roast chicken dinner began to be served, Artem broached the reason they were there.

'So, you want help. For what?'

'We want to find a safe place to live, away from Corporation,' began Jed, but his wife interrupted him.

'Gaia wants us to help her. We need to cross the ocean, spread the news that the planet has begun to heal. Remove the yoke of Corporation. Spread her message of renewal and new life.' She faltered as she realised everyone was gazing at her. 'She told me she needed us.'

'Is not hard to get you over there. I have plane. Will be hard to make point. Lots of space - not lots of people and Corporation have many eyes.' Artem shook his head. 'Will be difficult.'

'Have you been over there?' asked Jed. 'Can you tell us what it's like?'

'No, only flown. But skies are clear.' Artem grinned. 'I know place. I take you.' Then he frowned and steepled his fingers, pursing his lips before speaking again. 'Is not same. Is wilder, bigger, more space and more danger. But the cities, they still there. Not glitter like 9. You been 9?'

Jed, Martha, Dina and Max nodded sadly while Zac grinned then realised he was the only one and hastily took a sip of his drink.

'Does that mean New Corporation is fully in control over there?' asked Martha.

'I think in cities, yes. They should have tech and med and Collection - all things.'

'So where are they getting their babies from?' asked Ruth. 'We shut down the baby lab in 42.'

'Is not only lab, *milaya*.'

'What do you mean, it's not the only lab? There are more?' Kira was aghast. She looked at Jed in horror who half shrugged. He had no idea there were more labs.

'Is big world, yes?' Artem gazed around the table. 'You only met me today. Be more surprises tomorrow.' He chuckled at his own cleverness but when he realised no-one else was laughing, he grew serious once more. 'Listen, when you shut your baby lab you put Corp in panic. These babies sell for high credit. You stop Corp credit. This is very bad. Why they punish 15. So sad.' Artem shook his head. 'Now we have new New Corp and you lady, you pissed them off.' Artem wagged a finger in Martha's direction. 'These new neural implants, this is not what tech should be. All sheeps bleating, baa! Baa! Baa!'

No-one knew what to say but Artem didn't seem to notice. He continued.

'Med labs. That's how they do it.'

'How they do what?' asked Dina.

'Make the babies! They gather all the sperms and all the eggs then it's mix, mix, mix and bingy bangy bongy babies.'

'What in the Med Centres?' Martha was incredulous. 'Are you sure?'

Artem nodded vigorously.

'What about the sterilisation though?' Martha asked.

'Is cocktail. They dose you in water. But you know this - you broke water in 42, yes?' Artem looked back and forth for confirmation.

Dina nodded. 'Yeah, we found out they were treating the water but, are they doing that everywhere?'

'Yes! But they can undo it with sperms and eggs. Sneaky, sneaky, sneaky.' Artem shrugged as if it were a small thing but the others were shocked. This was something that even Martha's father hadn't known about, if he had been telling the truth.

Jed tried changing the subject. 'What about the force behind City 15? Do you know who that was?'

'Is militia.'

'New Corp have a militia?' Jed wanted to know more. 'Do you know where they are based? What their set up is like?'

'Is ghost. No chitter chatter.' Artem looked downcast then grinned again. 'But once they speak, I know.'

'How have they managed to build a militia without

anyone noticing?' Martha asked, addressing Jed.

'Well, the chief thought they never disbanded to be honest.'

'Is true,' Artem piped up. 'In beginning Coalition think problem - problem is genes. They no good. Event cause sickness and genes, no good. So, if people have babies, babies no good. This very bad. They make cocktail and sterilise and think we grow little bit and all is fine, all is okay.' He stopped talking and the whole room waited for him to continue.

'And?' prompted Ruth.

'And nothing. Stayed same. Babies grown, is what it is. What you're going to do?' Artem focused on his dinner and for a while no-one said anything while they processed what they'd learnt.

'I have a question.'

Everyone turned to look at Zac in surprise, not expecting him to have anything to add.

'Why don't they have the tech to grow their own babies over there?' he asked Artem.

'Is good question. Power. Power and technology. Is what Corporation have.' He paused to take a long drink. 'Over there is big place. Spread out. Harder to connect than here. Everyone sterile and everyone desperate for baby. Desperate means do anything, pay anything, give anything. And so, Corporation provide. They also destroy.'

'We know,' muttered Ruth.

'You think control here is control. Control there is air.'

'Is there any place for us over there?' Kira asked. 'It sounds like we'd be better off staying here.'

Artem was quiet and he looked at Zac who nodded briefly.

241

'The Resistance will take you. And I take you to the Resistance.'

'Oh, that's wonderful!' gushed Kira feeling relieved, turning to smile at Martha and the others. Martha started guiltily; she had not mentioned Zac's revelation about the Resistance to anyone else yet.

'For a price. Is business,' said Artem.

Silence fell as everyone turned to look at Artem.

'Yes, there must be price. Artem never does business without price.' But he seemed to be embarrassed and cleared his throat several times before continuing. 'I want to meet Gaia. I want to see mother of Earth. You show me and I fly.' He sat back in his chair, waiting to see what would happen.

Everyone turned to look at Kira this time. She flushed under the scrutiny.

'Um, we can't conjure Gaia up, you know? She is the spirit of the Earth. She only shows herself when she wants to,' Kira said tentatively, unsure as to how Artem would react.

'But you've seen her. You, all seen.' Artem looked around the table.

'Well, yes. But not all at the same time.' Kira's gaze flitted to her friends, looking at them to help her out.

'I saw her in the street but unexpectedly,' offered Jed.

'I saw her in Camp Eden,' said Max.

'And she sat next to me on a bench,' Dina chipped in.

'I saw her in the park,' said Martha softly, a faint tremor in her voice.

'Yes,' said Artem, pleased. 'You all see. You tell her to see me.'

Kira didn't think she had much of a choice. 'I'll see what I can do,' she said faintly.

No-one spoke much after that, eating their dessert in

silence and withdrawing to the next room for coffee. It wasn't until they split up into smaller groups that Jed cornered Kira and asked her the obvious question.

'How exactly are you going to get Gaia to appear?'

'I don't know. Try to reach her spiritually, I guess. I'm assuming this place has some kind of natural garden.' Kira glanced around, but it was too dark outside to see. 'I think it's a problem for tomorrow. The children are tired, I'm tired. I think a decent night's sleep would do us all the world of good.'

Kira and Jed made their excuses to the group, taking Peter and Grace with them to their guest room. Kira had no idea how she was going call Gaia forward but the moment her head hit the pillow she was fast asleep.

Chapter 30

Kira awoke to birdsong. Through the open window she could smell fresh grass after rain. The sun peeped through the curtains casting golden rays across the floor. She stirred slowly and realised was not there. The children were gone too. That shocked her into being fully awake. She leapt out of bed and grabbed a nearby jumper, chucking it on over her jumpsuit before hurrying out of the room. As Kira reached the top of the stairs, she heard laughter from the dining room and felt instant relief. On entering she saw she was the last to wake and everyone else, including all of Alpha and Beta team, were already seated and having breakfast. She smiled self-consciously and hurried over to Jed.

'Morning, love.'

'Morning,' she replied, giving him a quick kiss before going to grab a cup of coffee.

'So, today we meet Gaia, yes?' Artem spoke to Kira.

'Um, yes, we can try. Do you have a garden?'

'I have big garden. Herbs, plants and wild space.'

'That would probably be best.' Kira felt too nervous to eat anything. 'Can you take me there? We might as well make a start.'

'Do you want some company?' asked Ruth but Kira

shook her head and stood waiting for Artem. He kissed Ruth on the cheek which surprised everyone and then beckoned to Kira to follow him out of the French windows.

The gardens were beautiful, perfectly sculpted and full of heady perfume, but it was towards the bottom that Artem led Kira. He ducked under a hedge bower and stood to one side to let Kira take in the wild garden. It was stunning. Completely overgrown, full of every wildflower imaginable and bees, there were bees buzzing from flower to flower collecting nectar.

'Oh, this is perfect,' exclaimed Kira softly.

Artem stood expectantly, waiting for Kira to work her magic but she didn't know what she should do. She took a deep breath and tried to connect with the environment around her, but Artem's presence was off putting. Kira bent down to take off her socks and let her bare feet connect with the earth beneath her. She took another deep breath and tried to imagine blue energy from the Earth rising through her feet, travelling through her body and leaving the top of her head. At the same time, she visualised all the bad things that she'd been holding onto being swept out of her aura. After a good twenty minutes or so she felt relaxed and at one with the Earth around her, she thought she could sense Gaia and opened her eyes in hope but there was nothing there. Artem had adopted a lotus position on the ground to her right and he looked at her with hope in his eyes.

'I'm so sorry, Artem. I don't know what else to do. We could try lighting some candles and calling out for Gaia to appear, but I thought this would work.'

'Is okay. You tried. You stay and you try. Gaia come, then we go.' He helped her up and started walking back to the dining room while Kira processed what he'd said. If she couldn't summon Gaia, then Artem wasn't going to take them across the ocean. He also wasn't going to let them leave either. Her heart sank at the impossible task before her.

In the dining room everyone had gone except for Ruth. Artem left the two women together shouting over his shoulder that he'd talk to them later as he walked out the room.

'How did it go?' asked Ruth.

'Shouldn't I be asking you that?' countered Kira.

Ruth blushed. 'We're just old friends, reacquainting ourselves, that's all.' She nodded towards the garden. 'I gather it didn't work?'

'Oh, Ruth. I don't even know what to do! She's always sort of appeared before, hasn't she? I tried to connect with the Earth and open myself to her spirit. but nothing happened. And Artem...'

'And Artem what?'

'He said it didn't matter and I could try again, and we would stay until I did it.'

'Okay.'

'No, you're not listening, Ruth. He won't let us go until I've made contact, until Gaia manifests. We could be here forever!'

'I'm sure he didn't mean that,' Ruth replied but she looked worried. 'Let me speak to him.'

'Thank you. We can't stay here indefinitely, can we?'

Ruth shrugged and the women left the dining room in search of their children. They found them playing in a small sandpit around the side of the house.

'How'd it go?' asked Jed but Kira shook her head.

The day passed and there was no sign of Gaia. That evening as they went in to dinner, Kira hurried over to Ruth.

'Did you speak to Artem yet?' she asked, but Ruth shook her head.

Artem displayed the same jovial manner despite the muted response from the rest of them. Only the children were in high spirits earning themselves indulgent smiles and the odd laugh from the grown-ups. Once everyone had eaten and the families had left the dinner table, Kira managed to corner Ruth again.

'Well, are you going to speak to him?'

'Yes, but not right now!' Ruth muttered and turned away from her friend, smiling at Artem who was cooing over Sarah.

As the evening dragged on, Kira grew more and more restless; passing on her irritability to Grace and Peter until even Jed begged her to sit down and relax. She noticed Artem and Ruth whispering in the corner and was hoping her friend was managing to persuade Artem to help them anyway. At one point he shook his head vigorously but somehow Ruth made him smile again. Finally, Artem stood up.

'Goodnight one, goodnight all,' he announced as he left the room whistling. Kira darted over to her friend.

'Well?'

'He's agreed to take us, but he wants to wait until the morning before he announces it. He didn't want to but...'

'You convinced him!' Kira said happily.

'I agreed to stay.'

'You what?' Kira wasn't sure she had heard her friend correctly.

'I agreed to stay. Last night Artem asked if I would like to stay with him, here at his home and I told him I'd think about it. I was going to come with you, Kira, to the ends of the Earth if that's what it took, but this is the price for Artem to take you over the ocean. Me staying.'

247

'Do you want to stay?' Kira didn't like the idea of her friend being forced to do anything she didn't want to.

Ruth nodded shyly. 'I do. Sarah loves it here and Artem makes her laugh. She's never going to meet her real dad, Kira, and this feels like somewhere I could call home.' Ruth bit her lip pensively and looked at her friend. 'Is it alright with you?' she asked.

Kira could feel the tears springing into her eyes as she hugged her friend. 'Of course it's alright. It's not like we'll never see each other again.' The two women were laughing and hugging so much that Martha, Dina and the others came over to see what all the commotion was.

'Ruth is staying here and Artem is going to take us in his plane, no charge,' explained Kira.

'Are you sure you're alright with that, Ruth?' asked Jed.

'Yes, yes I am. I'll miss you all though.' There was more hugging and exclaiming over what had happened until Martha changed the subject.

'Has anyone seen Zac?' she asked.

'He was at dinner,' replied Jed. 'But he didn't come back in here. I think he wanted some time to himself.'

'Oh, okay,' said Martha, a little disappointed.

It was Jean who finally chivvied everyone to bed, and they were all still chattering happily as they ascended the staircase and went to their respective rooms.

The next morning, Artem was waiting for them in the dining room. He was practically bouncing on his toes in excitement. Once they were all gathered for breakfast he began to speak.

'I have announcement. Gaia came to me. To me! In my garden, she walk, and she touch flowers. Bees buzz. And I see her. I see Gaia! In my garden!'

248

'Oh, Artem. That's wonderful!' said Kira. 'What did she say?'

'She say nothing. But she came and after I say we go and so I know, we go. Is good to go.'

Everyone began talking at once until Jed banged the table with his cup for a bit of silence.

'Alright, I know you're all excited but listen, now is the time to decide whether you want to come or whether you want to stay. And believe me, it's fine if you want to stay.' He looked around the room to make sure everyone realised he was being honest. 'I'm going,' he said and then he sat down and looked at his wife.

'We're going, Grace and me and Peter.' Kira turned to look at her parents.

'We're staying, love. Artem's been telling me about some new medication he can get for my condition and anyways you don't want us two oldies gadding around with you. No, we'll stay here, won't we, Malcolm? And then when you've finished adventuring you can come back and tell us all about it.' Jean beamed at her daughter who smiled back. It felt like the right decision to Kira as well.

'I'm going!'

'And me,' smiled Max, holding Dina's hand.

The attention of the table fell upon Martha, Ash and Zac.

'Well obviously Lucas and I are coming,' said Martha.

'Yep, I'm in. You'll need a good techy,' said Ash which left Zac.

Zac looked at Artem for a long time before slowly nodding and turning to address Kira and Jed. 'I'll come too.'

'I fly, we all go. Is good.' Artem was smiling hugely

and there was an air of festivity about the room.

No-one was thinking about where they were going and what was actually going to happen. It wasn't until later when Kira and Jed were packing up the gear in their room that they began to talk about what it was they were doing.

'Are we going to be alright, Jed?' Kira asked.

'With regards to what, love?'

'Going in a plane with some mad Russian, across the ocean to join some Resistance we've never heard of to try and spread the word of Gaia, an earth spirit that hardly anyone has ever seen and who nobody knows how to contact!' She finally stopped for breath.

He stopped what he was doing to give her a hug. 'I reckon we're about to find out.'

~The End~

Thank You

Thank you for reading The Gaia Project, I really hope you enjoyed reading the second instalment to The Gaia Collection. I would be so grateful if you could review the book on Amazon and Goodreads and let me know what you thought.

I want to say a special thank you to my wonderful team of beta readers - CH Clepitt, Donna Tyrrell, Hannah Bligh, Debbie McGowan, Amy Leibowitz Mitchell and Simon Leonard. Your comments were invaluable, and you gave me the courage to 'kill my darlings'!

I couldn't write without my fabulous husband, Kevin, so a huge thank you to him. He listens to all my mad ideas, is always the first to read the manuscript and helps me figure out the tricky parts.

Finally, I have to thank the brilliant Ian Bristow for creating another superb book cover for me.

About the Author

Claire Buss is a multi-genre author and poet based in the UK. She wanted to be Lois Lane when she grew up but work experience at her local paper was eye-opening. Instead, Claire went on to work in a variety of admin roles for over a decade but never felt quite at home. An avid reader, baker and Pinterest addict Claire won second place in the Barking and Dagenham Pen to Print writing competition in 2015 with her debut novel, The Gaia Effect, setting her writing career in motion. She continues to write passionately and is hopelessly addicted to cake.

Sign up to Claire's newsletter for exclusive content and all the latest writing news: http://eepurl.com/c93M2L

Follow Claire on Twitter: @grasshopper2407
Like Claire on Facebook: facebook.com/busswriter
Visit her website: www.cbvisions.weebly.com

The Gaia Solution
(Book 3 in The Gaia Collection)

Kira, Jed and their friends have fled New Corporation and joined the Resistance, but their relief is short-lived as they discover how decimated the human race has become and learn of an environmental crisis that threatens to destroy their existence. Kira and Jed must travel up the mountain to the New Corporation stronghold, City 50, to bargain for sanctuary while Martha and Dina risk everything to return to City 42 and save those who are left. With the last of her reserves Gaia, the fading spirit of the Earth uses her remaining influence to guide Kira and her friends but ultimately, it's up to humanity to make the right choice.

Available at your favourite book retailer.

Printed in Poland
by Amazon Fulfillment
Poland Sp. z o.o., Wrocław